His Ultimate Desire

Joy Avery

HIS ULTIMATE DESIRE

First print edition: May 2015

DEDICATION

Dedicated to the dream.

CONTENTS

ACKNOWLEDGMENTS

My thanks—first and foremost—to God for blessing me with this gift of storytelling.

As always, to my husband, Marcus and daughter, Avion— thank you for your unwavering support and patience. I love you both very much! You both believed I could, so I did! And I keep doing.

A huge thank you to an awesome critique partner, Lyla Dune. Check out her Pleasure Island series. It will have you laughing until your stomach hurts.

To my friends and family who've offered tons and tons of encouragement and support, I express my greatest gratitude. Thank you for being in my corner.

Chapter 1

"It's a madhouse out there," Marisol Chesapeake said, joining her aunt Vaden in the kitchen of Lady V's diner. She dragged her forearm across her sweaty brow. "You're lucky you're on a first name basis with fire chief, or else you'd be shut down for exceeding your occupancy limit."

Vaden laughed. "Take a break, sugar. You've been going at it all evening. I know you're about to drop."

Yes, she was. In hindsight, three-inch heels was probably not the best footwear choice she could have made. Her feet felt like they were about to detach from her body and run off on their own. In her defense, she hadn't planned on waitressing. But she'd grin and bear it. There wasn't anything she wouldn't do for the woman in front of her, including tie on an apron and play happy hostess as she'd done as a young girl.

"Anything for you, Auntie." Marisol draped her arms around the portly woman's neck and kissed her cheek.

The top of Vaden's head came to Marisol's chin. With skin the color of dark brown sugar, eyes a shade lighter, and a head full of thick, black hair, Vaden possessed a regal beauty that beckoned attention. Which she got plenty of.

Marisol's gaze slid across the kitchen to Baxter—the only cook Lady V's diner had ever employed. Was there something going on between those two? If so, they deserved the reward for best kept secret in Indigo Falls.

The thought didn't linger long. Something so juicy wouldn't have gotten past Ms. Ernestine—Editor-in-Chief of the Indigo Falls Gazette, self-proclaimed blogger extraordinaire and biggest snoop in town. Nothing got past Ms. Ernestine.

Marisol could see the headline now: THERE'S MORE THAN BACON SIZZLING INSIDE LADY V'S DINER. She chuckled to herself.

Vaden swatted Marisol away. "Go on now, child. You see I'm working."

Vaden liked to pretend she didn't enjoy all of the affection Marisol and her brothers lavished on her, but Marisol knew deep down she did. "But you shouldn't be working. It's your birthday. You're supposed to be relaxing."

"Quit your fussing over me. I've relaxed plenty of birthdays."

"Yeah, Pixie, quit your fussing and take a break. You're not used to all of this manual labor."

Marisol shot a scowl at her brother, Jacen, standing behind the prep table chopping green peppers. Like all of the Chesapeake men, Jacen was handsome. Skin the color of nutmeg—smooth and flawless—strong features, and towering stature. And also like the other Chesapeake men, an eligible bachelor.

Marisol shot him the bird, then cringed when she remembered Vaden's presence. Respect for your fellowman was of the utmost importance to Vaden. And as expected, she chastised them both.

"Quit picking at your sister, Jacen Chesapeake," said Vaden.

"Yeah, Sheriff, quit picking at your sister," Marisol mocked.

"And you, young lady," Vaden said, shifting her attention back to Marisol. "Unless you're hitchhiking, keep your fingers out of the air. You weren't raised in nobody's woods."

Marisol pouted playfully. "Yes, ma'am," she said like a scolded six-year-old. Sometimes she did feel more like a tot than an adult. Inevitable when you were the youngest *and* the only girl.

Marisol poked her tongue out at Jacen before loading up and heading out the door again.

"Hey," Jacen called out before she'd escaped.

"What, big head?" she asked, eyeing him over her shoulder, a wide grin on her face.

"Love you. And I'm glad you're finally home."

Marisol had never played favorites with her brothers, but at that moment, Jacen claimed the title. "Ditto, Sheriff. On both counts."

When she moved from the room, Marisol blinked back the tears threatening to fall. Yep, she was glad to be home.

"Jesus," Marisol said, noticing that even more people

had packed into the diner in the short time she'd been in the kitchen. The residents of Indigo Falls, North Carolina still loved to gather. It thrilled her to know that hadn't changed in the years she'd been gone.

She hadn't lost her touch, steadying the plates in her hands with as much precision as she handled a scalpel in her examining room.

Her examining room.

The life she'd recently abandoned filtered into her thoughts. Her job as a forensic pathologist would be the only thing she missed about leaving Charlotte. Definitely not the man she'd fled from. Shaking away the thought, she focused on the task at hand, the fork-tender pork chops she carried.

Thursdays signaled the popular "chop night" at Lady V's Diner. People drove for miles just to get a taste of the succulent meat smothered in homemade brown gravy and onions. But tonight, the walls were bursting at the seams, because Vaden Chesapeake also celebrated her sixty-fifth birthday. The entire town had come out to celebrate the woman who'd been a rock to many of them.

Shimmying her way through the droves of people, she placed two of the plates in front of eager patrons. Breathing in the aroma of fresh bread, herbs, and sautéed onions made her stomach growl. Man, she'd missed the smell and taste of down-home southern cooking. The chatter and laughter of family and friends and forks clanking against plates washed her in warmth she hadn't experienced in far too long.

Marisol surveyed the rustic diner. Individuals were

4

crammed into the solid black booths, while others overflowed at the square tables, clawing like crabs for one of the black upholstered chairs so they'd no longer have to stand. The sight made her giggle.

Pictures—some framed, others a simple print tacked in place—covered almost every inch of the walls. The snaps captured images of the town, patrons, and the many celebrities who'd visited the renowned diner. One photo in particular caught her eye and slowed her steps.

Kincaid Tinsdale.

A wave of something soothing coursed through her, and a smile touched her lips. It'd been three years since she'd seen him last. Much longer since they'd been a couple. Ten years, to be exact.

Something else flowed through her, but this current wasn't as calming. Perhaps it stemmed from her recalling their last encounter three years ago. The one that'd spiraled out of control, resulting in the two of them in the backseat of his Ford F-250.

That night he'd reminded her of what pure pleasure felt like. That passion still rocked her to the core anytime she allowed herself to bask in the memory, which she'd done a lot since returning home.

The tingling between her legs forced her to snatch her eyes away from the image of the two of them locked in a passionate embrace. Luckily, she wouldn't have to worry about another lapse in judgment. Kincaid was hundreds of miles away.

Dismissing the thoughts of her first love, she searched the room for her best friend, Rayah. She'd promised the woman they'd hangout once Marisol had finished helping with the crowd. That'd been three hours ago.

Once Marisol caught sight of her, Rayah mouthed something she couldn't quite make out. Marisol squinted as if doing so would help her decipher Rayah's words. *Behind me*? Tossing a glance over her shoulder, Marisol came close to losing the two remaining plates she held.

Kincaid?

A breath seized in her throat as an instant attraction awakened her entire body.

What was he doing there? The last she'd heard, he'd been stationed on an offshore oilrig in Louisiana. Her heart rate increased and a knot tightened in the pit of her stomach.

Starting at his close-cut coal black hair, her eyes glided over all six plus feet of him. The five o'clock shadow gave him a rugged appearance. A damn good look on him, if you asked her. At thirty-eight, he could easily pass for years younger. She attributed it to good genes.

Time hadn't changed him much at all. He was still the most attractive man she'd ever laid eyes on. Taut muscles stretched the fabric of the black polo shirt he wore and dark relaxed-fit jeans hung perfectly from his well-toned frame. His skin appeared to have a hint more chocolate-hue to it. It only made him that much more appetizing.

The breath she'd been holding captive seeped out slowly through her partially open mouth when Kincaid's lips curled into a smile. Marisol baulked at the thought of how those lips had once been able to make her body quiver. When her nipples hardened and the throbbing between her legs became too intense, she wanted to sprint away, but her feet wouldn't budge. Her heart pounded against her ribcage with each step he hazarded toward her.

"Marisol Chesapeake," he said, his penetrating gaze roaming over her face.

In that moment, she wondered if he, too, was recalling their night together. Then again, why would he? She was sure that night had stopped meaning anything to him a long time ago—if it'd meant anything to him at all. That night had been the result of two people needing a release. And boy had he released her...over and over again.

"It's good to see you," he continued.

She stood frozen, her words lost on the sheer allure of the man in front of her. The man with whom—at one point—she'd been prepared to spend her life with. Snapping out of her stupor, she said, "*Kincaid*. H...how have you been?"

He eyed her awkwardly for a beat before responding with, "Good. And you?"

Yes, she heard and understood the question, but her brain wouldn't process an appropriate response. Someone bumped Kincaid from behind, forcing him a hair closer to her. The scent of his cologne—the one that'd always driven her insane with desire—encircled her like a vengeful spirit, taunting her in the most pleasurable manner imaginable.

"Great," she finally managed to blurt. "I've been great." She lifted the plates. "Busy."

His gaze held firmly to hers. One corner of his mouth lifted into a half-smile. "I see."

Those lips. Fight it, Marisol. Fight it. Someone called

out to her, jolting her back to reality. Before Kincaid's presence could wreak further havoc on her body, she said, "It was good seeing you." For a minute she thought he hadn't heard her, because he just stood there silently staring at her.

"You, too," he finally said, something dangerously appealing flashing in his eyes.

Halfway across the room, Marisol heaved a couple of deep breaths. This was bad. Real bad. She'd be the first to admit her lingering attraction to Kincaid Tinsdale. Any woman with a heartbeat would be captivated by him. His magnetism drew you in deeper and deeper the longer you were in his presence. But was her body supposed to respond to him like this?

She wrangled another deep breath, then released it slowly. This was ridiculous. At thirty-five-years-old, why was she running from her ex-lover like some inexperienced adolescent? She was a Chesapeake. Chesapeakes didn't scuttle away; they faced their problems head-on.

Chancing a glance in Kincaid's direction, their eyes locked. A jolt of something she couldn't label overloaded her system, making it impossible to breathe, let alone turn away. Until their connection, she hadn't considered it warm inside the diner. But now, it felt as if her body was melting from the inside out. The summer temperature had nothing to do with her dissolving body. If Kincaid had experienced the same climate shift she had, someone would soon have to extinguish them both.

Bad. Real bad, she repeated to herself.

Kincaid's stern eyes bore a hole straight to her core.

Feelings she'd long buried came rushing back with the vibrancy of an unmanned train. How could he still command such a response from her? Such a reaction signaled one thing... *Trouble*.

She made a mental note... Maintain a safe distance from Kincaid Tinsdale.

Chapter 2

After returning to town from his roofing job in Charleston, South Carolina mere hours earlier, all Kincaid had truly wanted to do was take a hot shower and curl up in his own bed for a change. No such luck. His brother, Mason, had been so damn insistent on him attending Vaden Chesapeake's birthday celebration that Kincaid had delayed the rest he needed and dragged himself to Lady V's.

Now he understood Mason's urgency to get him there.

When he'd first spotted Marisol weaving through the crowded room, he'd chalked it up to his eyes playing tricks on him. Possible, since he hadn't gotten much sleep lately. But nope. There she stood. Pretty damn real.

It made sense she would take a break from her bigwig doctor's life to attend her aunt's celebration. They were close. What didn't make sense was why she'd just treated him like some random Joe in the streets. They'd shared a life together, once. More than a life. They'd shared love. And lots of it.

Memories he'd done so well at expelling came crashing down on him with a vengeance. Their eyes locked and everyone else in the crowded diner disappeared. He no longer heard the cries of fussy babies or the elevated tones of loud talking seniors. It became all about him and Marisol; the only woman he'd ever given his heart to.

Kincaid clenched his teeth when he recalled the circumstances of his and Marisol's split. He'd loved that woman in a way he'd never dreamed possible, but it hadn't been enough to keep her from shattering the foundation they'd built. Even now, as they stared across at each other, he could feel that familiar pull. He couldn't understand how after all of this time his heart still ached for her.

Remembering their last encounter caused tightness at his crotch. No matter how hard he'd tried, he hadn't been able to forget how it felt to be deep inside of her. The cries for more. The sweet sound of his name rolling off her tongue.

Dammit, he cursed the memories.

The longer he eyed Marisol, the warmer the room grew. She was even more beautiful than he remembered. She'd changed, but not in a bad way. Instead of the short hairstyle she'd worn in the past, her brown hair now cascaded over her caramel-toned shoulders.

She'd gained a little weight, about ten pounds—if he had to guess—but in all the right places. Her breasts strained against the white blouse she wore, and those thighs... He longed to be those burgundy Capri pants pressed snuggly against her ass. Her runway-ready legs seemed even longer in those sex-me heels. If he had his way, sexing her is exactly what he'd spend the night doing.

The familiar hunger that only Marisol could stir—and quench—forced him to snatch in a deep breath, which did little to curtail the throb in his boxers. Clearly, his body also remembered how good she could make him feel in the bedroom...kitchen...hallway...

Marisol's best friend, Rayah, said something that drew Marisol's attention away from him. Damn Rayah for severing their connection, even if she had done him a favor.

It wasn't until the connection had been lost that he realized how potent his desire for Marisol still remained.

"Hey, hey," Mason said, clapping him on the back.

Kincaid winched from the contact, kneading at his stiff shoulder.

"My bad, man. Your shoulder still bothering you?"

"Yeah," Kincaid said. He hoped the ibuprofen kicked in soon.

"You should really see a doctor." He smirked and glanced in Marisol's direction. "What do you know, a doctor."

"I can't believe you set me up like this. My own brother, plotting against me. You knew she was going to be here, didn't you?" Kincaid asked, his focus remaining steadfast in Marisol's direction.

"Well, it is her aunt's celebration, so, yeah, I guess I had an idea."

An idea, huh? Sounded like total BS to him, but he let it ride...for now. One thing for sure, staring across at her eased the fatigue in his muscles. "Is she visiting for the week or something?" Kincaid asked, not wanting to appear overly interested, despite the fact that he was.

"Or something. As of a month ago, she is a permanent resident of Indigo Falls. She's staying with Vaden until she finds a place. Or so I hear."

Permanent resident? How was that possible? Well, he knew how it was possibly, but what would prompt her to leave Charlotte for small town living? It didn't make sense. His fingers dug into the tightness in his neck, completely knocked off balance by the news. "You could have mentioned it to me."

"And ruin the surprise?" Mason nudged him. "Call this payback for the stunt you pulled in the woods with me and Nona."

Kincaid massaged his neck every time he thought about that day he'd pretended to be a madman at their campsite, there to kidnap Nona. Mason had nearly snapped his neck.

"Wow," Mason said.

Kincaid faced Mason with furrowed brow. He should have been pissed as hell at him for not giving him the heads up before coming here, but he wasn't. He'd never been able to stay angry at his brother for long. "Wow, what?"

"The two of you in the same town again... There's bound to be some trouble." Mason jostled him forward. "Go talk to her, man. You two have a lot of catching up to do."

Kincaid fiddled with the glass he held. "I tried. She darted away like I'd been gnawing on a garlic clove." He scanned as much of Marisol as he could that wasn't being blocked by the creep attempting to chat her up. A twinge of jealousy roused him, despite Marisol not being a part of his life for a very long time.

"You two were good together."

"Yeah, we *were*."

Occasionally, Kincaid allowed himself to recall their life together. There were days when he needed just a glimpse into his past with her. Others when he couldn't bear to look into the portal of their past. Then there were the times when he had absolutely no control over it. When his memories were triggered by a smell, or a sound, or even a face passing in a crowd. At those times, every single detail about her flooded his mind, right down to the expressions on her face as they made love.

Kincaid chortled. "She still looks amazing." Words he hadn't necessarily meant to express out loud.

"Were you hoping she'd gained a hundred pounds and lost all of her hair or something?"

Even if she had, she would have still been the most beautiful woman in the world to him. He'd seen far beyond her exterior. He'd seen the woman who would do anything for the ones she loved. "No, but..."

Mason shook his head. "Tony said he couldn't wait to meet the woman capable of making an honest man out of you. I wish Tony were here right now." Mason slapped a hand on Kincaid's shoulder, then apologized when Kincaid grunted.

Tony was Mason's best friend, and like a second brother to Kincaid. Like Mason, Tony had also found his soul mate. The man was absolute proof that playboys could be reformed. "If he were here, it would be a wasted trip."

Mason eyed him, a serious expression on his face. "Who do you think you're fooling? There's clearly still a spark between you and Marisol. Who knows, maybe you two will find a way to rekindle that old flame."

That was a joke. He was sure Marisol's taste in men had sophisticated well beyond the point of loving a small town roofer from her past. Besides, one important aspect still remained. Kincaid took a sip of the watered-down lemonade. "She walked away from me, remember?"

Mason wrapped his arms around Kincaid's neck. "Anything's possible, baby brother. I'm living proof. Soon, I'm marrying the woman I love more than life itself. The woman who, in a few months, will give me the most precious gift any man could receive. A child." Mason shook his head as if he were in disbelief of his own fortune.

They both shifted their focus to Nona. Before much longer, Kincaid would be an uncle. He smiled every time he thought about it, as well as when he recalled the fact that his niece would bear the name of their late mother. Abigail Tinsdale. That little girl had some big shoes to fill.

"You're truly blessed, big bro," Kincaid said, meaning every syllable of it. "And I'm hella happy for you."

If Mason had been able to surrender his heart again, after everything he'd gone through in his first marriage, *anything* truly was possible. Kincaid laughed to himself. Who was he kidding? Him and Marisol? A couple again? *That'll never happen*.

A second after the thought, his mother's voice rang in his head. "*Never say never*," she used to say. He hated to admit it, but his mother would have been wrong about this one. Never was a pretty safe gamble for him and Marisol.

Not that he cared or anything, Kincaid asked, "Is Marisol seeing anyone?" Then realized what a silly question it'd been. She'd only been in town for a short time. But when Mason tensed slightly, it peaked Kincaid's curiosity. He shifted toward his brother. "Is she?"

"I...ah...saw her in the ice cream shop with the guy with the big ears. The one who runs the insurance company. Overcharging people for shoddy coverage. I don't think it's anything serious, though. She didn't look too overjoyed to be there with him. Downright bored, actually."

So she was seeing someone. The idea rubbed him raw. Okay, maybe he did care...a little.

"Remember what you told me a few years back?" Mason asked, snatching Kincaid from his thoughts.

He had a good idea of what his brother was referring to, but he said, "Refresh my memory."

"That if you ever got a second chance with Marisol, you would take it." He glanced in Marisol's direction. "Well, from where I'm standing, this looks very much like that second chance to me. I guess the question of the day is...what are you going to do?"

What was he going to do? That was a damn good question.

Chapter 3

Marisol narrowed her eyes, scanning the dimly lit room for Rayah. Though Marisol had been content spending another Saturday night on the couch watching reruns of *Good Times*, Rayah hounded her until she'd agreed to meet at Merle B's—Indigo Falls' local watering hole. Plus, she hadn't exactly forgiven Rayah for not informing her of Kincaid's move back to The Falls, as many dubbed it.

And speaking of Kincaid, this had better not be some veiled attempt by Rayah to get the two of them in the same room again. The idea screamed ridiculous, but she wouldn't put it passed the woman who still held out hope of them getting back together.

Kincaid.

His presence a week ago at the diner still rattled her. She'd avoided him ever since. Unfortunately, she hadn't been able to avoid him in her dreams. Dreams that'd caused her to wake panting and in a sweat.

Ugh. Kick him out of your system.

Scanning the aged establishment, Marisol noted the place hadn't changed much at all. Exposed wood stained a deep mahogany color gave the open space a quaint feel. At the extended teak wood bar, customers drank—and told lies—as Merle B would put it.

In front of the stage, where most nights welcomed a live band, individuals danced as the DJ played a mix of R&B and golden oldies. If things truly hadn't changed, at ten p.m. sharp, there would be a full hour of ballads by Otis Redding.

The "Big O" hour, Merle B called it. *To get lovers in the mood*," she used to say. Marisol glanced at the wall clock. In thirty minutes, she'd discover if the tradition still rang true.

Spotting Rayah at a highboy table in the back—entertaining as usual—Marisol ambled toward her, but slowed her steps when she got the eeriest feeling that she was being watched. A scan of the room revealed nothing, so she chalked it up to paranoia.

"There's my girl," Rayah said as she slid off the tall chair with outstretched arms.

Rayah stood an inch or so taller than Marisol's five-eight frame. Her green eyes sparkled as she donned a wide smile. The strapless, shimmering gray mini dress she wore showed off her long, caramel-toned legs and highlighted a figure most women would kill for.

Rayah released her and introduced the two men lounging at the table. "I want you to meet, Isaac and...*Garret*, right?"

The man nodded.

Both men were attractive, tall, and well-built. Personal trainer types, if she had to label them. Isaac was a lighter complexion, while Garret had more of a pecan tone. These weren't faces she recognized.

The one Rayah had introduced as Garret eyed Marisol in a peculiar way that made her a bit uncomfortable. His eyes slid to the cleavage peeping from her black strapless top and, boldly licked his lips. That gave her a good idea of what he was all about. And she wanted no part of it.

Creep.

Marisol rolled her eyes away from him and eyed

Rayah. Pointing over her own shoulder, she said, "I think I'm going to get a drink."

"I got you," Garret said, his dark cat eyes raking over her body. "What are you drinking?"

Ha. Allow him to get her drink and lace it with God only knows what. No, thank you. She flashed her palm. "That's not necessary. But thank you just the same."

Garret didn't protest, though the grimace on his face suggested he wanted to. The sour expression melted into a frown as he shrugged and set his attention to the dance floor. Probably prowling for less cumbersome prey.

"I'll go with you," Rayah said.

"No. Stay and entertain your guest. I'll be right back. Can I get anyone anything?"

Rayah and Isaac responded with a no, but Garret refused to even acknowledge Marisol's offer. Did he think his cold-shoulder treatment would force her to beg for his attention? She barked a laugh to herself as she trekked away from the table.

Had she really given up an evening with kid *Dyn-o-mite* for this? Sliding onto one of the rickety stools at the bar, she released an exasperated sigh.

"Hey there, baby cakes. What you doing sitting there all alone? Did my daughter brush you off for some Poindexter?"

Marisol smiled in Merle B's direction. The woman was tall—easily six feet and some inches—built like an ox and as strong as one, too. At sixty-four years old, she put fear in men half her age. Especially the ones who didn't know she had a heart of gold and wouldn't harm a fly...unless you screwed with two things: her livelihood or her Rayah.

"No, she didn't. I don't feel much like entertaining."

"Well, baby, looks like you're not going to have much of a choice." Merle smirked, looking past her.

Before Marisol could rotate on the chair, the scent she knew all-too-well met her before his words did. Fine hairs prickled her skin and heat warmed her cheeks.

"It's kind of odd how we keep bumping into each other."

Her coming face-to-face with Kincaid again was inevitable, but she hadn't expected it to be so soon. She collected a breath before rotating to face him. Staring up into his eyes was akin to smashing face first into a spotless glass window. You didn't recognize the danger until it was too late.

Kincaid wore a pair of black slacks and a black button-down shirt. Two of the top buttons of the shirt were undone and the sleeves were rolled up, revealing powerful forearms. Something about a man dressed in all black screamed sexiness. Something about *this* man dressed in anything, tantalized her.

Marisol's smile melted and she swallowed hard. So much of him, so close, was too demanding. Drawing in a slow breath, she fought to steady her rattled nerves. Rubbing the side of her neck, she said, "Really?"

Their gazes held. Kincaid's eyes combing over her face didn't startle her. Them settling on her mouth did. She shifted in her chair. After a second or two more, his eyes climbed to hers. Under his scrutiny, whatever coolness she'd conned herself into believing she possessed vanished, replaced by the scorching heat of uneasiness. She thanked God for the intrusion that came.

"Kin...caid *Tinssss*dale," Joe Otis slurred.

Joe Otis was tall and lanky with skin the color of worn leather. When sober, he was one of the best mechanics in Indigo Falls.

Joe Otis brushed his hand across Kincaid's shoulder. "Good, lawd, have mercy. You open-casket sharp. You sho' 'nuff taking somebody's daughter home with you to...*night*." He snapped his long, ashy fingers. "*Look out—*"

Joe Otis stopped abruptly, as if Marisol's presence finally donned on him. Or it could have been that he thought *she* was the one Kincaid would be taking home. He could definitely erase that notion from his thoughts. Go home with Kincaid? An iceberg had a better chance of forming in the center of town before that happened.

Joe Otis smiled at Marisol. "If it ain't little Pixie Star. Ain't so little no more, are you? Look at'cha. Pretty as a Shetland pony. You have any trouble out of any of these fools 'round here, you just let ole Joe Oat know. I'll take care of 'em."

"I will," Marisol said, smiling at the man who used to give her shiny nickels for the candy shop when she was a young child.

Joe Otis returned his attention to Kincaid. As they chatted, Marisol took the opportunity to steal a close assessment of Kincaid. Watching his lips move as he talked shouldn't have been so damn erotic. The smell of his cologne shouldn't have caused pressure between her legs. The way he stood—arms folded across his chest, flashing taut bicep muscles at her—shouldn't have caused her to pull her bottom lip between her teeth.

Squeezing her legs together did little to stop the pounding at her core. She chalked the reaction up to the natural response a sexually deprived woman had to a very attractive man, and not to the fact she had firsthand knowledge of the pleasure Kincaid was capable of dispensing.

Truth be told, there hadn't been another man who'd come close to pleasing her in the manner Kincaid had. Not that she'd had a great deal to compare him to. She'd only been with one other man. Her ex certainly hadn't been concerned with her sexual fulfillment.

"Here, baby. I think you need this," Merle B said in a delicate tone behind her.

Marisol swiveled and accepted the martini glass filled with an amber-colored liquid. "Thank you," she mouthed and emptied the glass in one gulp.

The cocktail hit her instantly, and her head spun for a second. How could she have forgotten that Merle B never watered down her drinks? The concoctions—what tasted like a blend of pineapples, coconut, and banana— supercharged the throbbing between her legs. Merle B was known for brewing up so-called "sexual elixirs." Had she just been dosed?

Kincaid finished up his conversation with Joe Otis, then slid on the stool next to her. "So, where were we?"

His tone—smooth, casual, confident-as-hell— unnerved Marisol even more. She shifted to face him. "I believe you were trying to convince me that you're not stalking me," she said. Where in the hell had that come from?

Kincaid tilted his head back and released a sexy laugh. Even his laugh captivated her. This was simply a mind-over-matter thing. Instead of thinking about how appealing Kincaid was, she needed to focus on his not-so-sexy features. Like his— Wait, that was sexy. Maybe his— No, that was sexy, too. *Ah-ha*. She had it. Those dimples. Those unattractive, deep-set dimples that...pierced those chocolate cheeks every time he smiled in that panty-wetting way he smiled. Very similar to the way he beamed at her now.

Trouble.

"Momma Merle, can I get a refill, please," she said, yelling down the length of the bar like a mad woman. Marisol met Kincaid's inquisitive eyes. "You should try one. It's really dicklicous—" Her eyes widened in shock. "*Delicious*. It's really delicious." She yanked her gaze away from Kincaid and briefly eyed the exit.

"It was nice seeing you at the diner the other night. Then you disappeared. If I didn't know any better, I would have thought you were avoiding me."

Marisol released a shaking laugh. "Avoiding you? Why would I have been avoiding you?" Yep, she'd avoided him.

"My thoughts exactly. Seeing how there isn't a reason for us to shun one another, right?"

Marisol eyed him sternly. Was he kidding? Did he really believe they didn't have a reason to avoid one another? Clearly, he'd forgotten about what'd happened the last time they were this close. He obviously wasn't experiencing the same tug she was. Then again, why would he? She was simply someone from his past. "Right," she finally said.

Kincaid continued, "I'd really wanted to catch up with you."

"That was a week ago, Kincaid. If you'd *really* wanted to catch up, you'd have stopped by my aunt's house and done so, *right*?"

Kincaid smirked, then glanced up at Merle B when she placed a drink down in front of Marisol.

"What's your poison, good-lookin'?" Merle B asked Kincaid.

"I'll take a Yuengling," he said.

"Such a creature of habit." Marisol stiffened. *Please tell me I said that in my head*. She had her answer when he responded.

"If it's not broke, why try to fix it?" Kincaid propped his elbows on the counter, then leaned forward. "I'm surprised to see you with something stronger than an orange juice. You've never been much of a drinker."

"People change," she said.

They held each other's gazes for a beat. In those moments, Marisol felt an unusual rush of confidence.

"You look good, Marisol. Great, actually. Even better than I remember. I would've doubted that was possible."

"Then your memory is bad. I'm ten pounds heavier." *Jesus*. Why did this stuff keep slipping out? She brought her glass to her lips. After this one, maybe she shouldn't have anymore.

"It's settled in all the right places," he said.

Marisol gagged on her drink, coughing ferociously. Kincaid slid from his stool and stood DNA close to her. The heat radiating from his body raised her temperature to a dangerous level. And when his hand rested on her back and glided up and down—grazing her bare flesh—there wasn't an inch of her that wasn't awakened by his touch.

Her coughing subsided, but her aroused state grew to a downright embarrassing degree. She felt like an alcoholic who'd just blown thirty-six months of sobriety. An absolute lush who couldn't stop drinking in every ounce of Kincaid. Then there was that woozy feeling that washed over her each time he ogled her with those menacing brown eyes. *Jesus*. It was time to say when.

"It was nice seeing you again, Kincaid. I should get back to Rayah and…" Her words trailed off. She inched off the stool, lost her balance, and slammed into his rock-hard frame. His arms closed around her, holding her snug against his warm chest. *Mmm*.

"Whoa. Are you okay?"

Marisol tilted her head and simply stared into Kincaid's eyes. If eyes truly were the portal to one's soul, Kincaid had to see the love she still harbored for him. "I hope you enjoy the rest of your evening," she said, pushing away from him.

"Dance with me," he said, capturing her hand before she could make her escape.

The warm sensation of his flesh against hers only dizzied her more. "Maybe next time."

"Is it too much for you to handle?"

Had he read her body language? She couldn't risk walking away now and allow him to claim some unstated victory. Plus, he knew better than anyone that she never backed down from a challenge.

Wait a minute. Had that been what he'd been banking on with his on-point accusation? Marisol reclaimed her hand. "Goodnight, Kincaid," she said, and ambled away.

From experience, she knew he wouldn't fight for that dance. He would simply watch her walk away, just like he'd done so many years ago.

Creature of habit, she repeated to herself.

***

Kincaid chuckled. So Dr. Chesapeake wanted to play hard to get. Maybe she'd seen through his word trickery, but that didn't matter; he wasn't letting her get away that easily. Not this time. Before the night was over, he intended on having her in his arms. And soon...in his bed.

The thought put a warm heat in the pit of his stomach. There'd been no other woman who'd fulfilled him like Marisol—sexually or otherwise. He had to know if her body still responded to his like it had in the past. It was one hell of a selfish motive, but she would get something out of it, too. A brief reminder of what she'd given up.

Brief?

The understatement of the year. Once he had her tangled in his sheets, he'd make sure there was nothing *brief* about their lovemaking.

"You're afraid," he called out, stopping her in her tracks.

Marisol rotated and barked a laugh. "Afraid?" She

backtracked until they were directly in front of one another. "Of *what*, might I ask?"

"I'll give you some time to figure that out." He took one last sip from his bottle and placed it on the counter. This time, he was the one sauntering away.

Three. Two. One.

"Let's dance," she said, brushing past him and leading the way to the dance floor.

Kincaid smirked. Seems he wasn't the only creature of habit.

The second Kincaid guided a seemingly uncertain Marisol into his arms, Otis Redding's "Chained and Bound" sounded from the ceiling mounted speakers. He didn't need to glance at his watch to know what time it was. Ten p.m. sharp.

They swayed slowly, side-to-side. After a minute or so, Marisol relaxed in his arms, her body melting more into his chest. Maybe this hadn't been such a good idea after all. How'd he allow himself to forget just how good she'd always felt in his arms?

The heat they generated intensified Marisol's delicate fragrance—a mix of floral and sweet. This close to her, he recalled how he used to steal kisses in the area where her jaw and neck met while they made love. There was something so damn sensual about that tender part of her body. And then there was the way she would squirm under him when he dragged his tongue across the delicate spot.

"Some things never change," Marisol said in a low tone.

For a moment, her words intrigued him. What did she

believe hadn't changed? Their undeniable connection? The sexual tension that'd always existed between them? The way his body summoned hers? His thoughts were doused quickly.

"Merle B's hour long Otis Redding tribute," she said.

"Have I given you enough time to figure it out?" he asked, searching her eyes.

Marisol swallowed hard before saying, "What...exactly is there to figure out?"

Were they really going to play this game? Who did she think she was kidding? He wasn't the only one privy to what was happening between them. The tension was too potent to ignore any longer. "I can't take this," he said.

"Take what?"

"You in my arms. Your mouth so close to mine. Me not taking the opportunity to kiss you senseless."

Two or three breaths passed between them before Marisol spoke. "Is this the moment I'm supposed to admit I want to kiss you, too?"

"There's no need." By the way her eyes kept sliding to and from his lips, he had a good idea she did.

"Good. Because I don't."

Kincaid dipped his head forward. "Are you sure about that?" He expected her to reel back, but she didn't.

"Very."

"So if I pressed my mouth to yours right now, parted your lips with my tongue, and kissed you until you panted, you wouldn't kiss me back?"

"N...no," she said in a shaky tone, "I wouldn't."

"Uh-huh." He searched her eyes. "Do you remember

what happened the last time we were this close?"

Marisol's eyes darted away. "Vaguely."

"In that case, let me remind you." He lowered his voice. "The backseat of my truck. Your legs pinned to your chest while my tongue—"

"Oh, that time," she said, nonchalantly. "The one where you took advantage of me in my inebriated state."

"Is that how you remember it?"

"There's no other way to remember it. I had a little too much of Merle B's spiced eggnog."

Ah, a case of selective memory. He bet she'd told herself that lie so many times that she actually believed it. "You had less than a half a glass of eggnog and a watered down Sprite. What I remember about that night is you screaming my name as you came multiple times." He also remembered her labeling what'd happened between them as a mistake, then fleeing away from him. He'd make sure there would be no escape for her this time.

Marisol swallowed hard. "How would you know how much I had to drink? I—"

"Because I watched your every move that night."

Marisol's brows furrowed. "Watched me? Why?"

"I wasn't alone. Every man in the building was admiring you." And it'd made the blood in his veins flow like hot lava. "The way that clover-green dress hugged your curves. How those gold, dangly earrings drew attention to your beautiful neck. How those four inch heels made your legs look like they went on forever."

Something tender flashed in Marisol's eyes right before she said, "You remember all of that?"

"I've been holding on to that memory for the past three years. I remember everything about that night. *Everything*. In grave detail."

"So it seems," she said.

Looking deep in her eyes, he said, "Tell me you don't feel it. The other night at the diner. Over at the bar. Here in my arms. Tell me you don't feel that tug. That familiar heat that has always burned so hot between us."

Marisol's lips parted, but nothing escaped except a warm breath. He had a strong temptation to glide the tip of his tongue across her bottom lip, then kiss her until her knees buckled.

"Say something," he said.

"I... What—"

Before she could complete her thought, Rayah interrupted their tender moment.

"Hi, Kincaid." She didn't wait for him to speak, which was a good thing because he would have probably growled at her. "Marisol, our friends would like to take us for *pancakes*."

"Pancakes?" Marisol asked absently, her eyes still locked on Kincaid's.

Rayah put her hand under Marisol's chin and rotated her head toward her. Speaking slowly, she said, "*Yes...pancakes*."

With clinched teeth, Kincaid watched awareness flash on Marisol's face. Was pancakes a codeword? Marisol eyed him tenderly, as if she actually harbored reservations about parting from him. His body begged her to stay, but a beat later, she stepped out of his arms. It took everything in him to let her go.

"Thank you for the dance," she said in a hushed tone.

There were unresolved issues between them, unanswered questions. But instead of mounting a protest, he smiled and nodded. "My pleasure."

Watching Marisol stroll away, Kincaid found minute comfort in one thing... The fact that he knew she wanted him just as much as he wanted her.

Chapter 4

A thousand questions danced around in Marisol's head as she trailed Rayah across the dance floor. The main one, why did she long to run back into Kincaid's warm, protective arms? She willed herself not to glance back at him, even though she could feel his eyes burning into her back. She could also feel that tug he'd alluded to. The one that had her so damn confused that her head spun.

She groaned. So much for the mental note to maintain a safe distance from Kincaid. Wrapped in his arms certainly couldn't be considered a safe distance. How insane could she be?

"That was close," Rayah said over her shoulder.

Marisol paid no attention to the woman's words. *A half a glass of eggnog*? Why was she remembering four or five glasses? Maybe she'd convinced herself of it to rationalize sleeping with Kincaid that night? *Jesus*. She was coming apart.

"You okay?" Rayah asked.

Marisol fanned her hand through the air and smiled. "Yeah. I'm fine."

Her thoughts veered back to Kincaid. His embrace contained more warmth than she'd experienced in months. She'd missed being held. *Truly* held. Held in a way that made her feel wanted, desired even. How could his arms still feel so comfortable, so familiar?

How did she explain wanting to lean in and press her lips against his? How did she explain the ridiculous level of desire that pooled in her stomach? How did she explain the scorching heat that'd coursed through her entire body when he'd all but dared her to deny wanting him?

All the unanswered questions made her head throb.

The fact that he'd been right irked her. *Tug*. She massaged the side of her neck. There was definitely a tug. A feeling she'd assumed had been one-sided. Now, she knew better. It didn't make sense. They could easily be classified as mere acquaintances, but their chemistry... As potent tonight as it had been when they were a couple madly in love.

Being with him felt as if the puzzle known as her life had found its missing piece. Being with him felt...normal. That scared her, because normal is what she'd been seeking. Finding it in his arms hadn't been what she'd expected.

Unable to stand it another second, she shot a glance over her shoulder. No Kincaid. A search of the room yielded no results. Where had he escaped to so quickly? *Damn*. She'd needed just one more hit of him. *The words of a true addict*.

"Marisol, are you even listening to me?" Rayah asked.

Shaking off the feeling of loss, she refocused her attention to her friend. "Yes, I'm listening." She paused. "What happen to your friends?"

"I don't know. They must've left when I came to rescue you."

Marisol's face contorted. "Rescue me? Rescue me from what?"

"That sexy beast known as Kincaid Tinsdale. He had

33

you all up and under his spell."

"What? You're insane."

"I have no doubt that you're going to end up in his bed—or his backseat—" she smirked, "but you can't make it too easy for him. I love Kincaid like a brother, but you need to make him work for it, work for you."

One beautiful dance with Kincaid didn't mean they were on the road to bouncing back to where they once were. And just because he'd made her heart thump—a little—didn't mean she was ready to let him back into it. Old wounds were still too fresh, still too raw. She couldn't handle being hurt again. Not so soon. Not by him. "No one's working for anything. We were just dancing. I'm not spellbound."

Rayah barked a laugh. "Girl, a minute more and the two of you would have been screwing in the middle of the dance floor. You know my mother doesn't allow sex in her place."

Marisol and Rayah both glanced at the NO SCREWING ALLOWED sign hanging high on the wall and burst into laughter. No doubt they were laughing at the same thing. The memory of Merle B catching two college kids getting busy in her storage room. Marisol doubted either would ever have sex again without seeing Merle B's brown face in their heads.

Calming her laughter, Marisol said, "Seriously, Rayah, there's nothing going on between Kincaid and me." Well, nothing she was willing to acknowledge right now.

"Okay. If that's your story..."

Maybe Marisol was deceiving herself. Something had

happened while she was in Kincaid's arms, but should she be breathing so much life into it? The more she thought about it, Rayah *had* rescued her. But not from Kincaid, from herself. It would have only taken him saying, "Let's get out of here," for her to have abandoned all commonsense... Again. Why in the hell did he make her so weak?

As if being summoned, Marisol glanced up to find Kincaid eyeing her from across the room. He stood with two other men. When he smiled at her, she returned the gesture. God, he was handsome. And solid as a rock.

Rayah snapped her fingers. "Earth to Marisol."

Slamming back to reality, Marisol said, "I'm sorry. I was—"

"Fantasizing?" Rayah gazed in Kincaid's direction and smirked.

"What—?" A shaky laugh escaped. "No, I wasn't." She kneaded at her earlobe. "I wasn't even looking at him."

Rayah arched a brow. "Really? Then tell me something, why were you moaning?"

Moaning? Jesus. Had she really moaned? "I was— I didn't— It's the delicious aromas wafting from the kitchen. I hummed *mmm*. I didn't moan. There was no moan." Her words had been delivered a bit too defensively to make them believable, especially by Inspector Rayah.

When Rayah laughed a bit too vigorously, Marisol scowled at her. "Whatever," she said. "I'm not fantasizing about anyone. Especially *Kincaid Tinsdale*."

Marisol shot a disapproving glance in his direction. One that morphed into an ogle of pure satisfactions when she took in another hefty dose of him. A beat later, she grunted and whipped her head away.

Rayah rolled her eyes away. "So delusional."

Marisol swatted playfully at her. "I still haven't forgiven you for not telling me he was back in town."

"*Ugh*. For the hundredth time, I didn't know. I knew he was in South Carolina working; I didn't know he'd returned."

Marisol was proud of Kincaid. He'd finally done it. He'd finally started his own business. It'd always been a dream of his. Marisol absently listened to Rayah as the woman went on and on about something. Her thoughts weren't as much on their conversation as they were on the man who stood less than twenty feet away from her.

"Besides, I thought you'd be long gone before he returned. You said you were only going to be in town two weeks," Rayah said.

This yanked Marisol back into the conversation. "Yeah, that's before I learned Patrick decided to tarnish my reputation as a result of me leaving him. He has a lot of pull, Rayah. I don't think I'll ever get another job in North Carolina. Not doing what I love, at least. I applied for a position in California, but I haven't heard anything yet. He's probably gotten to them, too."

Those who knew her well would never believe Patrick's allegations of alcohol and drug abuse, but the rumors would cause suspicion. What had she ever done to him to warrant such malice?

"Bastard," Marisol spat through clenched teeth.

"We're not going to dwell on that loser or any other negativity tonight. Tonight, it's about you, me, and as much

36

fun as we can handle. And besides, I love having you back in Indigo Falls. I hope you never leave. I'm sure I'm not the only one who feels that way." She cut her eyes in Kincaid's direction.

"You're a witch, you know that." Marisol hugged her friend. "But I love you."

"I love you more."

When she pulled away, Rayah's expression was condemning. "What?"

"Tell me the truth, you want to grab him and suck on him like a big ole chocolate tootsie pop, don't you?" She glanced in Kincaid's direction again. "I don't blame you. He does look good enough to eat. And his brother... If that man wasn't about to jump the broom..." She bit into her bottom lip and moaned. "The things I would allow him to do to me."

"Stop staring," Marisol said, a sense of urgency washing over her.

"You know Kincaid's still in love with you, right?"

The words stilled Marisol. What an absurd comment. Yes, he'd loved her once, many moons ago. Before she'd— Marisol crushed the memory of her ending their relationship. Not that she cared or anything, she said, "What makes you say that?"

"The fact that he hasn't had a serious relationship since you two broke up. *Ten* years ago. Plus the fact that he still looks at you like you're a flawless diamond. What is it he used to call you?"

Marisol chuckled softly and tore at the napkin she'd picked up. "His caramel fairy."

"That's right. His caramel fairy." Rayah grinned. "I love

it."

The fact that Kincaid was single did surprise her. Not wanting to seem too intrigued, she asked, "How would you know Kincaid hasn't been in a serious relationship? He's been in Louisiana for the past couple of years. For all you know, he could have a wife and kids stashed somewhere." The thought made Marisol queasy.

"You're the only woman who's ever held that man's heart, and you know that."

Something tugged at Marisol's heart.

Rayah's gaze slid away. "Can I ask you something, Marisol?"

Uh-oh. Marisol groaned, sure she wasn't going to like the direction this conversation was headed. "Would it matter if I said no?"

"Probably not."

She rolled her eyes to the ceiling. "Go ahead."

"Do you regret it, walking away from him?"

Every day of her life, but instead she said, "I've loved Kincaid since as long as I can remember, Rayah. I never thought he'd just let me go without—" The words stuck in her throat. *Without a fight*, she said silently to herself. When Rayah touched her arm, Marisol flashed a weak smile at her. "I gave Kincaid all of me. All he gave me in return was—"

"Thunderous orgasms," Rayah said.

That was one of the things Marisol loved about her best friend. She always knew how to lighten the mood. Marisol swatted at Rayah and laughed. "I'm being serious here." Unfortunately, she couldn't curtail the memory of how skilled Kincaid had been in the bedroom. Thunderous orgasms, indeed. "Can we focus on something other than what used to be?"

Things hadn't worked out for her and Kincaid in the past, could she really believe things could be any different this time around? Allowing any man back into her heart— even the one man she was sure could pump life back into it—was the last thing she needed to be thinking about.

As always, Rayah ignored Marisol's words. Playing devil's advocate, she said, "*Sooo*, does that mean you still love him? You said *I've* loved him and not something more past tense like I *used* to love him."

The question took her by surprise, so she used the only defense she could think to mount. "Are you forgetting about Harrison? We've gone on a few dates." She yanked at her earlobe.

"You went on two *dates*, and I use the term loosely. He stood you up on the third, remember?"

Yeah, she remembered. He'd all but begged to get her to forgive him.

"He took you to the ice cream shop, griped when you upgraded to a waffle cone—a mere *fifty cents* extra, mind you. Then he thought *you* were being unreasonable when you called him out on it. The man went all soft over *fifty lousy cents*. I bet Kincaid would have let you upgrade to a waffle *bowl* without raising a brow."

Marisol chuckled. "Shut up, Rayah." But Rayah was right. When they were together, if it made her happy, Kincaid was all for it. He'd spoiled her rotten, had treated her better than any man had ever treated her.

Rayah continued, "And didn't you tell me you asked for vanilla, but *Harrison* got you pineapple instead, because *he* thought you would like it better? He's already trying to control you." Rayah shook her head.

No threat of a love connection existed between Marisol and Harrison. He was nice enough—a bit too frugal for her taste—but nice. Plus, he smacked when he ate. She could never invite him to Sunday dinner at Vaden's. Smacking at her table was one thing Vaden didn't tolerate. She would have given Harrison a two-hour lecture on the proper way to chew, then probably tossed him out of the house.

Not to sell him short, Harrison would make someone a good catch. Unfortunately, that someone just wasn't her. And the fact that he didn't believe in sex before marriage definitely ruled him out.

All that aside, the controlling behavior he'd exhibited with the ice cream turned her off. Sure, it would seem petty to most, him changing her flavor, but for her, it raised red flags. She'd ignored those same red flags in her last relationship and, as a result, suffered months of hell.

Why had she agreed to go out with Harrison in the first place? Marisol debated the issue in her head. *Normalcy.* That was the only way she could justify it. She'd needed a sense of normalcy in her life. But using Harrison to achieve it had been wrong. Leading him on was worse.

"Are you going to answer me, or what? It's a simple yes/no question. Are you still in love with Kincaid Tinsdale? And be honest with me and yourself, Marisol Chesapeake."

She stared at her friend as if doing so would force the

woman to stand down. She knew better than to believe it would. "No," played on the tip of her tongue, but wouldn't take the plunge. Besides, it would have been a lie that Rayah would surely have called her out on.

Be honest with yourself. Advice she could have used years ago.

Searching out Kincaid in the crowd, Marisol sighed. In a tone not much louder than a whisper, she confessed. "Yes, I still love him." Loved him in a way that scared the hell out of her. She'd never stopped loving him, even after all of this time.

But wasn't that normal? Didn't your first love always hold a special place in your heart? Or was that just something women who couldn't let go told themselves?

Chapter 5

Kincaid waved at the woman propped inside the doorway watching Gabriel climb into the truck. When Marisol walked out of his life, he'd gone through a reckless phase, and her name was *Paige Tanner*. She was as reckless as one could get. Paige had wanted more, but he'd only been in it for the sex. She provided the escape he needed after losing Marisol.

His foolish period hadn't lasted long. Honestly, he'd only slept with Paige because she was Marisol's arch-enemy. It had been a bastardly thing to do, but at the time, he was so hurt, so angry, he hadn't given a shit about right or wrong.

Kincaid waited for Gabriel to climb into the truck. That little dude had given him a reason to calm his scandalous ways. He had to be a good role model for him. He was going to miss him like crazy when they moved to Atlanta in a few weeks.

Once Gabriel was all strapped in, Kincaid put the truck into gear and drove away. "What's up?" Kincaid asked.

"Not much. Got an A plus on my spelling test."

Kincaid held up his hand. "High five." Once they'd slapped palms, he said, "That calls for a celebration. Anywhere you want to go for lunch."

"Ms. Vaden's," he said without hesitation, then smiled revealing a missing front tooth at the bottom of his mouth.

Kincaid groaned to himself. *Anywhere but there.* After their interaction at Merle B's a week ago, he'd wanted to give Marisol some space. If he showed up at the diner, she would really believe he was stalking her, which couldn't be any further from the truth. Wanting desperately to see her didn't make him a stalker, right?

"You sure you want to go to the diner?" Kincaid asked as a last-ditch effort to sway the child. "We can hit Foley's pizza. Get you a huge slice of pepperoni pizza. Whatcha say?"

Gabriel considered the suggestion for a minute, pressing his slim finger into his chin and gazing upward. A beat later he shook his head. "Nah. I want the diner. Mr. Baxter makes the best cheese sandwiches ever."

Well, he was right about that. When he eyed Gabriel, Gabriel clasped his hands under his chin as if he was praying. "Pleeese," he said.

At nine-years-old, the kid had a good grip on manipulation. Kincaid caved. As if he had any other choice. "All right. All right. If it's cheese sandwiches you want, it's cheese sandwiches you'll get."

"Yes!" Gabriel pumped his tiny fist in the air.

This should be interesting. Kincaid eyed Gabriel. "Everything going okay at home?"

Gabriel shrugged. "Yeah. I guess. Mom goes to class at night. She's gonna be a fluff bottomless. She's always practicing. And studying. She makes me study with her. I never get to play my video game." He pouted and folded his short arms across his chest.

What the hell was a fluff bottomless? Was that some kind of stripper degree? When they'd messed around, Paige had been a stripper, but she'd given it up after she'd had

Gabriel. Was she at it again?

"Did your mom mention what a *fluff bottomless* does?"

Gabriel tossed his hands in the air and rolled his brown eyes to the ceiling. "They take peoples' blood. Everybody knows that."

Ah. A phlebotomist. "Oh. That kind of fluff bottomless. I thought you were talking about the other kind," Kincaid said.

Gabriel slapped his hand over his forehead and shook his head. "Oh, boy. Grownups."

Five minutes later, they pulled into the parking lot of the diner. One of the first cars he spotted was Marisol's black Acura. A part of him had hoped she wasn't there—the part that didn't want to be labeled a stalker, while another part—a much larger part—had hoped to get a glimpse of her.

He hadn't seen Marisol since the night he'd held her in his arms at Merle B's. The night he'd realized just how much he still loved her. He caught sight of her through the large window. Wearing a white T-shirt and what looked like jeans, she moved from table to table. Even from this distance, her beauty was undeniable.

Shaking off the feeling of euphoria, he turned to Gabriel. "Okay. We're here. Let's eat some sammiches."

"Yeah," Gabriel said, unfastening his belt and exiting the truck.

When they entered the diner, Kincaid instinctively sought out Marisol, but she was nowhere in sight. Maybe she'd spotted him and retreated to the back. He swept the diner once more before directing Gabriel to a booth near the back. A minute or so after sitting, they were greeted by a young girl he didn't recognize.

"Hi, I'm Harmony. Welcome to Lady V's. Our lunch specials today are..."

She flipped open a small, black notepad, but before she could locate the menu she apparently searched for, Kincaid said, "We're just going to take two cheese sandwiches."

She jotted it down on her pad, then asked, "What about drinks?"

Gabriel bounced up and down inside the booth. "I want a milkshake. Vanilla. No, chocolate. No, vanilla."

Kincaid and Harmony both eyed Gabriel as if they were waiting for him to change his mind again. When he didn't, Kincaid continued, "Lemonade for me."

Harmony smiled. "One *vanilla* shake for the cutie and one lemonade coming right up. I'll be back in a flash," she said, strolling away.

Kincaid was tempted to ask the girl about Marisol, but resisted.

"She's pretty," Gabriel said with a bounce of his thick brows.

"She's too old for you."

"Malik in my karate class said I should date older women. They're more mature."

Kincaid barked a laugh. "And how old is Malik?"

"Ten, but he doesn't date any woman younger than twelve."

Kincaid laughed again. "What does—?"

"Wow. She's really, *really* pretty," Gabriel said, staring wide-eyed past Kincaid.

Kincaid didn't have time to turn his head before he heard the sensual voice that made his body overly aware of how much he wanted her.

"Okay. One vanilla milkshake and one—"

By the expression on her face, Marisol was shaken by his presence.

"Kincaid?"

As if trying to exhibit a sense of confidence she didn't possess, she flashed a shaky smile. Her true state of nervousness was revealed by the sloshing lemonade in the glass when she placed it in front of him. Had the glass been completely full, the table would have been soaked.

"Hey," Kincaid said, willing his eyes to stay on hers and not roam down the length of her beautiful body. "We…ah…came by for a couple of Baxter's cheese sandwiches."

Marisol's eyes slid away from him and toward Gabriel. "Who is this handsome fella?"

"That's my boy Gabriel." Kincaid held out a fisted hand. When Gabriel didn't acknowledge it—too starry-eyed by Marisol's presence to notice—he said, "You gonna leave me hanging?" Gabriel tapped his small fist against his. "That's more like it."

Marisol whipped her head toward Kincaid, her eyes wide with surprise. "You have a son?"

"Yeah. And I'm ten," Gabriel said.

Kincaid witnessed the instant change in Marisol's body language, and questioning filled her eyes. Without putting in much effort, he could guess exactly what was racing through her head. "No, he's not my son. And you're nine," he said, eyeing Gabriel. Facing Marisol again, he continued, "I'm his mentor. The Raising Men Project sponsored by the church."

Kincaid watched as the tension in Marisol's shoulders eased. She looked relieved.

"Oh," she said, a hint of a smile on her face.

Their silent and awkward stares were interrupted by Harmony carrying two plates holding thick, gooey cheese sandwiches. Marisol jolted as if the awareness she'd been staring at him finally set in.

"Here you go," Harmony said, placing the plates down. "Can I get'cha anything else?"

Kincaid eyed Gabriel, who'd already torn into his sandwich, then back to Harmony and shook his head. Before Harmony had even walked away, his eyes settled on Marisol again.

"I'll let you two enjoy your lunch," Marisol said and made a motion to follow Harmony.

Without thinking, Kincaid shot his hand out and captured hers. Marisol flinched the second he touched her, but she didn't snatch away. Her eyes slid to their latched hands, then glided up to his eyes. Her expression—a mix of fear and uncertainty—was enough to cause him to drawback.

"We're going for sno cones after this. Will you join us?"

There were no plans to go for sno cones, but it was the only thing he could think up on such short notice. When

Marisol glanced at Gabriel's half-empty glass, he was pretty sure she knew it was all a ruse.

"Sno cones, too? *Yes*," Gabriel said. "This is the best day ever. Can we go by Ms. Faye's candy shop, too? I love, love, *love* her gummy bears. Especially the ones that taste like cotton candy. Can we go, please?"

Putting Marisol on the spot, Kincaid said, "Well, that's up to Dr. Chesapeake." He stared at her, waiting for an answer.

Gabriel's eyes widened. "You're a real doctor?" When Marisol nodded, he said, "Cool. Please, please, please come."

Marisol smiled warmly. "I don't think that's a good idea, sweetie." Her gaze returned briefly to Kincaid, then shifted back to Gabriel. But before she could say anything else, Gabriel cranked up the charm.

With puppy dog eyes and a gentle voice, he said, "Please go with us for sno cones. You'll love 'em, I promise." His hands spread wide. "They got like a gazillion flavors. Cherry, grape, banana. And they give you stickers. A puppy or a bunny rabbit or a smiley face."

Marisol chuckled, then folded her arms across her chest. "You're just too adorable for your own good. But I can't go, cutie. I'm working."

"I can handle things here, Marisol," Harmony said, approaching the table. She fanned her hand around the diner. "It's not like we're bursting at the seams."

"Yeah, Harmony can handle it," Kincaid said.

When Marisol faced him, he could see the mounting protest in her eyes. What excuse would she give next?

Probably something ridiculous like having to scrub the bathroom toilets, or clean a grease trap, or—

"Okay," she said, pointing over her shoulder. "Let me just run to the back for a second."

When Marisol strolled away, Gabriel performed a series of swift handclaps. "Oh, boy! The best day ever," he repeated.

Kincaid had to agree. It was shaping up to be a really good day.

Chapter 6

Marisol didn't regret being there with Kincaid, strolling down Ivy Lane like lovers. What she regretted was the feeling that she belonged there, by his side. And what she regretted even more was the scowl she'd given big booty Brenda when the woman eyed Kincaid like a piece of meat, as they strolled past her beauty shop.

Okay. It hadn't been *just* Brenda she'd leveled with her eyes. It'd been Brenda, along with the three or four other women who'd undressed Kincaid with their eyes. Why in the hell did she care that other women found him irresistible? She had no right to douse any of their fantasies. Heck, she'd had plenty of her own.

Marisol understood the women's fascination. Kincaid could send a ravenous need through any female. He was a constant reminder that rain wasn't the only thing that could get a woman wet. And his ability to rouse her with a brown-eyed glance frightened her. So, why in the hell was she here with him?

Kincaid called her name, snatching her out of her thoughts. Just watching his lips move excited her. When his arm brushed hers, she got chills. This was the first man she'd ever kissed. The first man she'd ever given her body to. He'd seen every inch of her from top to bottom. So why did being next to him make her nervous?

"You with me?" he asked.

"Yes." When he eyed her skeptically, she laughed. "I'm with you all the way."

He flashed a crooked smile. "How does it feel to be back in the house with Vaden?"

"I'm enjoying spending time with her. It brings back a lot of good memories. But, I have to admit, I will be glad when I get my own place. Vaden cooks a full breakfast every morning. All my clothes are fitting too tight."

Kincaid didn't comment, but the roguish grin on his face spoke volumes. Marisol continued, "I made an offer on this gorgeous bungalow. I fell in love with it."

"Lucky bungalow," Kincaid said, just loud enough for Marisol to hear.

Pretending she hadn't heard him, she swallowed hard and said, "Uh, it's a fixer upper, but my brothers have agreed to help."

"You're beaming. It must be a beauty."

She flashed a wide smile. "It's going to take some TLC, but it will be."

"If you need any roof work, just let me know. I know a guy who knows a guy."

"I may have to take you up on that...*guy*."

He eyed her in the way a lover would his mate, with admiration. Butterflies fluttered in her stomach. It reminded her of the way he'd looked at her so many times in the past. Even now, when they were no more than friends, she enjoyed the nostalgic feeling.

"Look at me. I'm flying," Gabriel said from a few feet ahead of them.

"Don't crash," Marisol said, pulling her eyes away from Kincaid.

"I won't. I'm a professional. *Zoom*." He smiled and

buzzed away.

"What's that?" Kincaid asked, pointing to a spot on her shoulder. When she glanced down, he brushed a bent finger across the tip of her nose. "Made you look. I can't believe you still fall for that."

One of the things she missed about Kincaid was his sense of humor. He'd always had a way of making her laugh, even at times when happiness wasn't on her radar. That wit had helped her survive the first couple of years of medical school. "You're so childish."

They shared a laugh.

"So, Dr. Chesapeake, what brought you back to Indigo Falls?" he asked.

Marisol stared off into the distance. If she lied to him, he would know. If she told him the truth—psycho ex—he'd pity her. She decided to give him a mix of the two. "There were cutbacks at the hospital. I had other opportunities, but I really felt like coming home. It's safe here," she said absently.

"Safe?" He slowed to a crawl. "Did something happen in Charlotte?"

When she turned toward him, his eyes were stern on her. A lot had happened in Charlotte, but instead of elaborating on it, she said, "No. It was just a figure of speech." She studied him to see if he'd bought any of it. Just as he could read her, she could read him, too. And all signs pointed to yes.

What she couldn't tell him, couldn't tell anyone— especially her family—was that she'd fled Charlotte like a thief in the night. The Chesapeake name was synonymous with strength. How could she—as a Chesapeake—confess that she hadn't had the strength or commonsense to leave a volatile relationship?

When a dog barked behind them, Kincaid rotated as if gunshots had rang out. A pug pranced up to them, tilted its head and stared. By Kincaid's reaction—squealing and pouncing onto a park bench—you would have thought it was a bullmastiff.

"Get your dog, ma'am," Kincaid said to the elderly woman holding the leash.

The woman shot him a look of pity, shook her head, then strolled away.

Marisol cracked up. "You're still afraid of dogs?" She laughed more.

Making sure the coast was clear, Kincaid jumped off the bench. "Once you've been bitten, you become very cautious. You were there. You witnessed the brutal attack."

Yes, she had been there, which is how she knew *attack* was a very colorful play on words. "Oh, yeah. I remember that. That Pomeranian would have eaten you alive had that little girl not saved you. What was she, four?" She snickered.

"Laugh at my pain," he said.

They continued down the sidewalk.

"I'm glad you decided to join us," he said.

"Like I had much of a choice. For the record, using a nine-year-old to do your dirty work was low." She flashed a smile to let him know that her words were playful.

"You're giving me too much credit. That was all Gabriel. I think he has a crush on you."

They eyed Gabriel walking about twenty steps in front of them, humming, with his arms still wide and flying. A child's ability to entertain themselves...

"He seems like a good kid," Marisol said.

Kincaid nodded. "He is. Smart as a whip, too. The kid can out-spell me."

"Honestly, you were never that good of a speller, Kincaid."

He nudged her and they both laughed.

"I'm just giving you a hard time," she said. "So, do I know Gabriel's mother?" The look on Kincaid's face—like he'd just slammed into a brick wall—told her she did. She stopped and rotated toward him. "Do I?"

Kincaid's jaw tightened. "Ah...yeah...you do."

When he didn't readily offer the name, she laughed, "Well?"

"Paige." He searched her face as if waiting for her to have some kind of reaction.

The name rang in her ears like a deafening chime. "Paige...*Tanner*?"

He nodded.

Paige had been her nemesis all throughout high school. The flirtatious woman made no secret of her crush on Kincaid. Always grinning and waving at him, even when he and Marisol moved hand-in-hand through the hallways of their high school. The things she'd done to entice Kincaid were scandalous: cornering him in the men's bathroom, flashing him with her breasts, offering him blowjobs. The list went on.

"*Paige*?" she repeated vaguely. She started to move

again. "How is she these days?" she asked, attempting to void her tone and expression of any emotion, despite experiencing a free flow of it.

"Good, I guess. Other than picking up Gabriel every other weekend, I don't have much contact with her."

Her attention drifted to the spot in the town square where she and Kincaid used to sit and enjoy ice cream cones, and where Paige would stroll by and wink at him. "Sorta sounds like parental visitation." *Damn*. She closed her eyes and groaned to herself, not meaning for the words to escape.

"I'm 99.997 percent sure he's not my son."

This time Marisol slammed into the brick wall. Stopping abruptly, she whipped her head toward him. "You...slept with Paige?"

Kincaid slid his hands into his pockets and stared at her, a pained expression on his face. His shoulders slumped and a second later, his eyes slid away.

The air escaped from her lungs. *Oh, God, he did.* Her heart sank. She rested a hand on her collarbone. Her lips parted, but no words escaped. *Breathe, Marisol, breathe.* The warm breeze she'd enjoyed moments before now burned like acid on her skin. *How could he*? Of all people, how could he have slept with Paige? Instead of simply asking, she chose the one option she was becoming good at... Running.

Marisol stopped. Massaging her earlobe, she said, "You know what," she pointed across the square, "I promised Rayah I would swing by her daycare and help her with something. It completely slipped my mind." Forcing a smile, she said, "Can I get a sno cone rain check?"

The manner in which Kincaid eyed her suggested he knew she had no intentions of honoring the request, but he didn't call her on it. Maybe he understood the hurt swirling inside of her. Maybe he could see the pain in her eyes. She didn't know, didn't care. The only thing that was certain...her need to escape.

"Sure. We'll walk you there," Kincaid said, a look of defeat on his face.

Marisol flashed her palm. "No. You promised Gabriel a sno cone and gummies. Promises should mean something. I'm sure he believed you. Don't disappoint him."

"Like I've just disappointed you?" he asked.

She wanted to scream, "*Hell, yes. Paige Tanner. You screwed Paige Tanner,*" but instead said, "How could you disappoint me, Kincaid? I've set no expectations for you."

Her reaction to the news was ridiculous, she knew. None of this should matter now, something that happened many years ago, but it did. And as hard as she tried, she couldn't shake the feeling of betrayal.

Kincaid slid a hand from his pocket, closed his eyes and pinched the bridge of his nose. "It was a long time ago, Marisol. I was—"

"Stop, Kincaid. Don't. You...you don't owe me any explanation. And you're right, it was a long time ago." But it still hurt like hell. She pointed over her shoulder. "I better get going."

"Rain check?" he questioned.

Staring up at him, so many questions swirled in her head. Had he and Paige been in a relationship? Had they been in love?

Marisol forced a crooked smile and nodded. "Rain check." She backed away, turned, and speed-walked through the square.

Chapter 7

As hard as she'd tried, Marisol couldn't purge the knowledge of Kincaid sleeping with Paige from her thoughts, which explained why at two o'clock in the morning, she was on the floor doing crunches.

"Eighty, eighty-one, eighty-two…"

Exercise always helped when she was in her feelings. So did eating. The smothered pork chops and bowl of mac 'n cheese she'd consumed at the diner earlier, along with the near gallon of sweet tea she'd washed it all down with, played in her head. Then there was the two slices of key lime pie she'd downed twenty minutes ago. She increased her momentum.

"One hundred."

Marisol sat up and rested her elbows on her bent knees.

Of all people, Paige? Marisol massaged the back of her neck. Why in the hell was she acting like she was still in high school? "I'm a grown woman, dammit."

She flinched when something struck her window. A grown woman who scared easily. Another *ting* sounded, and she lurched to her feet. Creeping to the window, she pulled back the curtain and peeped out. A gasp escaped before she squatted out of sight. Her body brutally reminded her of the lunges and burpees she'd done prior to the crunches.

What was Kincaid doing there, tossing rocks at her window as he'd done when they were teenagers? Her first instinct was to ignore him, but after another *ting*, she drew in a deep breath, released it in a long, steady stream, then cracked the window.

In a tone void of emotion, she said, "Kincaid, do you have a death wish? If Vaden finds you out there, squishing her award-winning petunias, she's going to fill you full of buckshot."

"I'll take my chances," Kincaid said. "I needed to see you."

"Why?" she asked, though it didn't take a genius to figure that out. One word… *Paige*.

"Come down." Under the glow of the full moon, his brown eyes twinkled. "Please."

"It's two in the morning, Kincaid. I'm in the bed."

"I can come up." He pointed to the ivy covered trellis.

Climbing the trellis may have worked when he was a scrawny teenager, she doubted it would hold him now, when he was full-grown and weighted down with muscles.

Against the nagging feeling in her gut, she said, "Give me a minute. I'll be down."

Kincaid bowed his head and kicked at the grass, just as he'd done when they were younger and she'd disallowed him entry. She smirked and pulled away from the window. Did agreeing to meet with him make her insane? Yes, it did.

Snatching a scrunchie from the dresser, she brushed her damp locks into a ponytail. She whipped out of her sweat-drenched shirt, then freshened up with one of the baby wipes she normally used to remove makeup.

Makeup?

Screw it. She didn't possess the energy to apply any.

Besides, she wasn't trying to impress Kincaid. Slipping out of her workout shorts, she replaced them with a pair of red cotton ones. The white v-neck T-shirt she pulled over her head fit a tad too snug around the breasts, but she decided to go with it anyway. Once she'd slipped on a pair of flip-flops, she headed out of the room.

Not wanting to wake Vaden, she tiptoed along the stairs.

The second she eased the front door open the scent of Kincaid's cologne rushed at her, stopping her dead in her tracks. An overload of her senses hadn't been anticipated this soon. She really did hate herself right now, for enjoying the scent so much. Fighting the urge to slam the door and retreat back up the stairs, she steadied her senses and commanded her feet forward.

Marisol wrapped herself in her arms. "Aren't you a little too old to be tossing rocks at my window?"

Kincaid chuckled. "You're only as old as you feel. That would make me twenty-one."

If that analogy were true, that would make her seventy-one and a half. After directing him to one of the four rocking chairs, she took a seat opposite him.

"You look great," he said, rocking back in the chair.

Really? Of all of the things he could have said, he chose to start off with a lie. "Thank you." Giving a quick scan of the burgundy T-shirt and black jogging pants, plus the absence of his truck, she said, "Did you jog here?"

"Yeah, I did. I couldn't sleep. I should probably be home in the bed. Gabriel wore me out." He laughed, but she didn't share in his amusement. "I took him to old man

60

Rutger's farm. He chased geese for an hour. Galloped after your brother's horses for another hour. Taunted the cows and sheep. That boy's a handful."

"That's what happens when you fill a child full of sugar. All of that energy had to go somewhere."

"Yeah, I guess." His eyes lowered to his fidgeting hands, then came up with urgency. "I'm having a house built."

"Really? That's great. I'm happy for you."

"Thanks," he said softly. "I'm going to be an uncle." He beamed at the spoken words.

How long did he intend to dance around the real reason for his visit? Playing his game, she said, "I'd heard that. Congratulations. I know you're very excited. You love kids."

"That was one of the things we had in common. Our love for kids," he said.

His words caught her off guard. The memory of the large family they'd planned—five boys and two girls—played in her head and weakened her resolve. "Yeah, it was," she said, a smile touching her lips.

Kincaid studied her a moment, then said, "Do you remember when you thought you were pregnant?"

The question transported her back to that panic-stricken moment, the fear still fresh in her memory. "Oh, yeah. I remember."

"You had a full-blown panic attack. Hyperventilating and all."

They could laugh about it now. At the time, she'd never been more scared in her entire life. But Kincaid hadn't formed one bead of sweat. He'd told her if she was pregnant, everything would be all right. No way did she want to be pregnant, but his words had calmed her, assured her that she wasn't alone.

Marisol rested her hand on her forehead. "I was petrified." She shook her head. "All I could think about was Vaden killing me and my brothers killing you."

Kincaid laughed. "I was scared shitless."

"What? You were? You seemed calm, cool, and collected."

"I had to be strong for you. But man, I was quivering in my shoes. I couldn't let you see me sweating. It broke me to see you so distraught. I needed you to believe that everything would be okay. Even if I wasn't so sure. But I was prepared to do whatever it took to support you and our child."

"You held me in your arms and said—"

"*We're just starting our family a little earlier than expected*," they said in unison.

Kincaid leaned forward and rested his elbows on his thighs. "Sometimes I wish I could go back in time and—"

"Of all people, why Paige, Kincaid? Why the one person who..." Marisol closed her eyes. "We weren't together. You were entitled to sleep with whomever you wanted..." Her eyes eased open. "But why her?"

Kincaid scrubbed his hand down his face. "Because you hurt me. And in my head, sleeping with Paige, I was hurting you back. It was stupid. It was immature. But losing you... I went through something. I lashed out."

Tears stung her eyes. "Thank you for your honesty."

She couldn't allow him to see her tears. Couldn't allow him to see how much she still reeled over him, over the past. She pushed to her feet. "It's late. We should probably say goodnight."

Kincaid came to his feet. "We never really talked about what happened between us, Marisol. Like, what ended a love that should've been forever?"

His words were calm and delicate, but she could feel the passion behind them. When he took a step closer to her, Marisol flashed her palms to ward off his approach. "Maybe it's best to just leave the past in the past, Kincaid."

"Your tears suggest otherwise. I believe the past is finally catching up with us. I should've fought like hell to hold on to you, Marisol. I never should have let you walk away. I was young; I was dumb; I was angry."

This wasn't a conversation she wanted to have on her aunt's porch, in the middle of the night, but after a decade, she deserved answers. "Why—?" Her voice cracked, and she swallowed hard to push down the painful lump that was making it difficult to speak. "Why didn't you fight for me? Why'd you just let me go? Why...?" She slapped her hand over her mouth to conceal a sob.

His jaw tightened as if he were grinding his teeth. "I was angry that you'd given up on me."

With those words, tears streamed down her face. "Given up on you? I would have *never* given up on you. I loved you more than life, Kincaid. I—I simply wanted more from you."

"More?" He laughed, but it lacked humor. A quizzical expression spread across his face, his brows furrowed and his lips parted, but no words readily escaped. A beat later, he said, "I didn't have more to give you, Marisol. You already had every single ounce of me." His features tightened as if he were attempting to contain his anguish. "Why wasn't that enough?"

No way was she going to shoulder all of the blame here. This time she took the steps forward and her tone rose. "And you had every single ounce of me, too. You were my entire world. No one could have ever loved you more than I did. All I wanted was— She had to stop a moment to collect herself, to get her emotions under control.

"All you wanted was what, Marisol?" His tone mimicked hers, and frustration poured from his words. "What else could I have possibly given you that you didn't already have?"

"Your last name, Kincaid." The words seemed to echo off of the house. "You could have given me your last name. I wanted to be your wife. I wanted to feel like more than just a replaceable part in your life."

Kincaid's nostrils flared. Matching the heat in her words, he said, "You would have been my wife, Marisol. I just needed time."

Marisol tossed her hands in the air. "Time for what?"

"Time to make sure I could give you the kind of life you deserved. One that would have assured I would've been able to provide for you and the large family I wanted with you."

Marisol wrapped herself in her arms, a wave of regret sending a cold chill crawling up her spine.

His tone calmed. "I just needed time. Time you refused

me. Losing you hurt like hell; still hurts like hell. But you know what hurt even more…?"

She wanted to place her hands over her ears and scream "No more." Wanted to admit that she wasn't sure she could take it. Before the courage materialized to do so, Kincaid continued.

"What hurt even more was the fact that you walked away and never looked back," he said.

The paralyzing sense of shame that washed over her made her limbs as heavy as lead. Her chin lowered to her chest, and in an exhausted tone, she said, "Kincaid—"

"A replaceable part in my life? No one could have *ever* replaced you. Woman, I loved you with everything I had. I loved you the only way I knew how. Completely. I cried over you. *I cried over you*," he repeated as if to make sure she understood the severity of his loss.

Marisol's body trembled, as she fought to hold back the flood of her looming tears.

"You ripped my heart out when you left me, Marisol." He shook his head. "You didn't need a piece of paper, you had my soul." He pulled his bottom lip between his teeth and glanced away briefly. When he brought his attention back to her, his eyes glistened. "*You* gave up on us. *You* gave up on me."

Before Marisol could respond, the front door swung open, and the unmistakable sound of a shotgun being cocked filled the air. For as long as Marisol could recall, her aunt had kept a shotgun by her bed, locked and loaded. Indigo Falls wasn't steeped in crime, but "*There was always the possibility*," Vaden used to say.

Marisol wiped at her eyes. "Auntie, it's me," she said, before the woman inadvertently let off a round.

With the shotgun still trained on them, Vaden squinted. "Pixie?"

"Yes, ma'am."

The weapon lowered to her side. "Child, what on God's green earth are you doing out here? You know I shoot first and ask questions later."

Marisol glanced at Kincaid, his eyes hard and cold on her. The fact that Vaden was there with a weapon didn't seem to faze him. In fact, she wasn't sure he was even aware of the danger he'd been in. She refocused on her aunt. "We were talking."

Vaden scoffed. "Talking? It sounded more like you were trying to round up cattle. I thought some drunkards from Merle B's had done made their way onto my porch. I nearly set it off out here."

"I apologize, auntie. I didn't mean to wake you."

Vaden pulled her hand to her hip. "That Tinsdale boy. I should've known."

Kincaid finally moved his eyes away from Marisol. "Sorry for waking you, Ms. Vaden."

"Well, since you're not a youngster any more, I reckon it don't make much sense to run you off. But you two keep it down before someone calls the law on you both. Do you really want to have to deal with your brother, Pixie? And Lord knows the mess you'll stir if Ernestine gets wind of this. It'll be all over that trash she calls a blog."

"I was just leaving," Kincaid said, his tone exhausted.

"Kincaid, wait," Marisol said.

As if she hadn't uttered a word, he moved across the porch, down the stairs, and disappeared into the darkness.

Chapter 8

"Baby brother, this is probably not the best time to remind you that you spent a thousand dollars on that crib. Especially when it seems you're having a love-hate relationship with it."

Kincaid glanced up from the crib he'd been attempting to assemble for the past three hours. Mason stood a few feet away, while Nona lounged on the brown leather couch. Both eyed him as if he were crazy, which was fitting because he felt like he was losing it.

"Sorry. Got a lot on my mind." He returned his focus to the fancy crib he'd purchased as a gift for his soon-to-be niece.

"Did they not offer assembly at the store, Kincaid?" Nona asked, making circles over her protruding belly.

Mason laughed, then answered for him. "Yes, they did offer *free* assembly. But Kincaid told the man *we* would do it ourselves. '*To makes sure it's done right,*' Kincaid told the man." He laughed again. "The man scowled and proceeded to inform Kincaid of the number of cribs they'd successfully assembled. In store and onsite."

Nona snickered. Kincaid eventually found the humor and laughed as well.

"The jerk failed to *inform* me it would be like assembling a vehicle," Kincaid said, allowing the wrench to fall from his hand.

When Nona made a hissing sound, he and Mason both eyed her with concern. Mason hurried to her side and knelt in front of her.

"What's wrong, baby? You okay?" Mason asked, placing his hand on her stomach.

Nona smiled and nodded. "Your daughter is fussy today. I think she's getting restless in here."

When Mason leaned forward and kissed her stomach, Kincaid couldn't help but admire them. He hadn't seen his brother this content in a very long time. Nona made him extremely happy. One day, he hoped to have what those two had.

"Get a room, you two," Kincaid said.

Mason eased on the sofa next to Nona. "What's got you so stressed, bro?"

Kincaid's jaw tightened, recalling the events on Vaden's porch. He didn't want to rehash all of the details, so he simply said, "Women are crazy."

"Hey," Nona said.

"You're excluded." He sighed. "Just every other woman in Indigo Falls. You're a transplant, so I guess you're immune."

"Any woman in particular?" Mason asked.

By the smirk on Mason's face, Kincaid had a good idea he knew exactly what woman he was referring to. Marisol Chesapeake.

An image of her tear-stained face flashed in his head. *Damn.* He'd allowed his anger to get the best of him. *His last name?* She'd ended their relationship because he hadn't asked her to marry him? That was the real reason she'd walked away? She'd given him some rinky-dink explanation about their paths veering in different directions. Their wanting different things. He should have known that was bullshit. If he hadn't spent so much time waiting for the perfect moment, things could have been so much different.

Damn.

All this time he'd been under the assumptions that she'd flat-out given up on him. It was feasible at the time. She'd already received her bachelor's degree and was working on a medical degree, while he'd barely gotten his diploma, had no steady job, and no idea of what he wanted out of life.

Back then, the only thing he'd known for certain was that he loved Marisol Chesapeake and would until the day he died.

"I don't know why you and Marisol are playing these games," Mason said.

"Speaking of Marisol," Nona said, "we bumped into each other at the bank the other day. She was upset about not having the offer she'd made on a house accepted."

With furrowed brow, Kincaid said, "The offer wasn't accepted?"

Nona shook her head. "She was heartbroken, too. But she's still looking."

A sense of sorrow washed over him. Marisol had her heart set on that place. He curtailed his thoughts before he became too invested. This was not his problem. After a lot of thought, he'd come to the conclusion that it was time for Marisol's reign over him to come to an end. His brain processed the words, but his heart didn't seem overly eager to accept them.

"I'm meeting with her soon. She wants me to take a look at her portfolio. Would you like for me to put in a good word for you?"

He chuckled. "That won't be necessary," Kincaid said. "But thanks for the offer."

Mason's cell phone rang, and he excused himself.

"Would you like some womanly advice, Kincaid?" Nona asked.

"Any insight on the inner workings of a woman is welcomed, so, yes, please. Y'all are impossible to figure out."

Nona laughed. "We're not a mystery. We just want to be loved, unconditionally. Plain and simple."

That was one thing he'd definitely accomplished with Marisol, loving her unconditionally. Kincaid remained silent as Nona stared across the room at his brother, her eyes full of admiration for her future husband.

"Sometimes when you least expect it, love stumbles into your life bringing with it the purest form of happiness ever imaginable. When you experience it, everything else takes a backseat. Fear, doubt, it all simply melts away, leaving you open and able to welcome back into your life the one thing that had hurt you so deeply in the past. *Love*."

Kincaid processed her words.

Refocusing, Nona said, "I'm sorry. Sometimes I lose my train of thought when I think about how in love I am with your brother."

"You two are lucky. You have something...special. I envy that. But I'm really happy for the both of you."

Nona cocked her head and eyed him a moment before

speaking. "Do you remember the first time you kissed Marisol?" she asked.

Was she serious? Heck, he remembered the date of every special moment he and Marisol had shared. The first time they held hands as boyfriend and girlfriend, the first time they kissed, the first *'I love you'*, the first time they made love.

"Judging by that smile, you're remembering a lot more than your first kiss," Nona said.

She was right. He would never forget the first time they'd made love. He wasn't a virgin, but Marisol had been. She'd wanted him to be her first. They'd driven to a place on the outskirts of town the locals called Firefly Landing. He'd lined the bed of his Chevy truck with dozens of plush pillows. They'd made love under the stars and the glow of hundreds of fireflies. At the time, he hadn't known shit about being romantic. Looking back, that night was the essence of romance. He longed to relive it.

"There's still a lot of love between you and Marisol, Kincaid. That much is evident. So, instead of quarreling on her aunt's porch, try discussing what's really going on between you two."

How'd she know about the argument? He hadn't even shared that with Mason. Apparently, she witnessed the questioning look on his face.

"I ran into Ms. Ernestine at the market. She mentioned it. She also asked if you and Marisol were dating again."

Ms. Ernestine took great pride in blasting people's business on her scandalous blog—The Walls Are Talking. The woman was better at sniffing out information than the government. One thing was for sure, if Ms. Ernestine knew about the argument, the entire town knew.

"What did you tell her?"

"Absolutely nothing. Mason warned me about her. Besides, she didn't need me to tell her that you and Marisol are still in love with each other and on the road to reconciliation." She smirked.

"I'm not in—" He paused. "She's definitely not in love with me. We just have a lot of history together. The night of the argument, we simply got caught up in the past."

Nona shook her head. "Despite what you want to believe, if she didn't still care deeply for you, nothing that happened in the past would matter in her present." Nona flashed a warm smile. "You still have a hold on her heart. You have to decide whether or not you want to let her slip away again. She's waited a decade for you, Kincaid. If you love her, don't make her wait another minute longer."

He mulled over Nona's words. Marisol definitely still had a hold on his heart, but did he still have some kind of hold on hers?

Chapter 9

Marisol sat at the kitchen table with a cup of coffee pressed to her lips, but she wasn't drinking the steamy brew. Instead, she stared trance-like out the kitchen window, focused on two lovebirds—or so she labeled them—perched on a tree limb.

She hadn't gotten a wink of sleep the last few nights, reeling over the things Kincaid had confessed to her. Through his eyes and his words, she'd experienced his pain. God, what had she done?

"Still thinking about that Tinsdale boy, I see," Vaden said, entering the room.

"No, ma'am." She witnessed the *child-do-you-think-I-was-born-yesterday* expression on Vaden's face. Marisol placed her mug down. "It's just that he still has the ability to get completely under my skin."

"Because you still love him. And he loves you. Two people don't go at it like you two did on that porch unless there is still a lot of lingering feelings."

Marisol released a shaky laugh. "I don't love Kincaid."

Vaden waved her words off. "Go on, child, and tell that to someone who don't know no better." Vaden lowered into the chair opposite Marisol. "When you're lying, you yank at your earlobe." Vaden pointed in her direction. "Like you're doing now."

Marisol dropped her hand into her lap. Did she really?

"I'm old, experienced, and I've even been in love a time or two." She laughed. "I know the signs. He was your first love. First loves tend to linger in your heart."

"Ten years?" Marisol asked.

"The real thing lasts a lifetime." Vaden stared off as if she were reliving a memory. She refocused on Marisol. "You were crushed when the two of you parted ways, but truthfully, I was happy."

Marisol scrutinized her aunt. "Happy? Why?" How could Vaden have found joy in her pain?

Vaden took Marisol's hand. "Don't get me wrong, child. I wasn't happy that you'd experienced such heartache; I was happy because you were so young and you needed to experience life beyond Indigo Falls. Beyond that Tinsdale boy. You ate, slept, and breathed him."

Although it was hard to hear, Vaden was right. Had she remained with Kincaid, she would have never spread her wings so wide. She never viewed their parting as a blessing, but in a way, she guessed it had been.

Vaden beamed. "Look at you now. You've traveled the world, become a highly respected doctor. I'm damn proud of you."

Marisol's eyes widened. Vaden rarely cussed, and when she did, it always took Marisol by surprise. "Auntie."

"Done a little cussing in my day, too." Vaden winked.

"I have you to thank, Auntie, for the woman I've become. You never let me give up on anything."

Vaden patted Marisol's hands. "You want to know a secret? I've always liked that Tinsdale boy. Even at such a young age I could see he truly loved you. Love like that doesn't die. It may hibernate for a while, but never dies. Don't deny yourself the happiness you deserve. The happiness you want." Vaden smiled. "Yeah, I see how you look at him. That boy holds your head and your heart."

The doorbell chimed and Marisol eyed the wall clock. Who was visiting at ten in the morning?

Vaden pushed away from the table. "Lord, this better not be one of those hovahs."

"I got it," Marisol said, pushing away from the table.

"Go on and finish your coffee. I'll handle this." A minute or two later, Vaden called out to her. "Pixie, you have a visitor."

"A visitor?" she mumbled. *Kincaid.* A smile touched her lips. When she rounded the corner, the smile faded. "*Harrison*? What are you doing here?" she asked as she neared the screen door.

Harrison stood board straight. In the proper manner he always spoke, he said, "Marisol, I need to speak with you, please."

What the hell was he wearing? "*O...kay.*"

When she joined him on the porch, he led her to one of the rockers. She thought about the night she and Kincaid had occupied the porch, then shook the sinking feeling away. Why did her thoughts constantly drift to him?

Harrison positioned a rocker directly in front of her, then took her hand into his. His palm felt like a damp sponge against hers. She eyed their joined hands. *Uh-oh.* This couldn't be good. Lord knows she couldn't take any more drama.

"I think we should take our relationship to the next level."

Marisol whipped her head upward. "Excuse me?" Had

she heard him correctly? Clearly not, because what he'd just said would suggest they actually *had* a relationship to take to the next level. A couple of trips to the ice cream shop hardly qualified them as a couple.

"I want us to go steady, be exclusive. I really like you, Marisol. And I know you like me." He rumbled off a robust laugh. "I mean, what's not to like? I own my own business, I'm in perfect physical health, and I'm rather pleasing on the eye, wouldn't you say?"

Marisol's eyes roamed over his golden skin and the thin strip of dark hair above his top lip. Complimenting himself really excited him, if his dancing hazel eyes were any indication. She could admit he was easy on the eyes, but... "Harrison, I—" Harrison's ears wiggled like a horse's, and she fought to hold back her laughter. When they wiggled again, she couldn't hold it any longer. A chuckle morphed into a fit of laughter. And she couldn't stop laughing. As hard as she tried, the laughter kept coming.

A puzzled expression flashed on his face. Marisol slapped a hand over her mouth to smother her amusement. But when his ears fluttered a third time, he reminded her of one of her brother's thoroughbreds.

"Marisol, what is so dang funny? I'm pouring my heart out to you here."

"I'm sorry, Harrison."

Look away, Marisol. Look away.

By the time she'd regained her composure, Harrison's skin was an intense shade of crimson. Bolting from the chair, she said, "Excuse me a moment." She didn't wait for his response before disappearing inside the house and sprinting toward the bathroom.

Collecting herself in front of the mirror, she headed back to where she'd left Harrison waiting. "I'm such an idiot," she whispered. Crafting an apology in her head, she sighed. There had to be a way to let Harrison down gently.

Marisol froze the second she pushed through the screen door. Harrison would have had to be blind not to witness her reaction to Kincaid's presence. A mix of shock and elation filled her. "Kincaid?"

"Marisol," he said, his lips twitching into a strained smile.

Her eyes slid to Harrison, than back to Kincaid. "Wh...what are you doing here?" she asked, forcing her feet forward.

He ignored the question. "Harris was just telling me—"

"Harrison." Harrison came to his feet, pushing his glasses further up his nose. "The name's *Harrison*."

Kincaid scanned Harrison's lime green and electric yellow biker shorts and matching spandex top. One thing she could say about Harrison, the man had no shame. Kincaid eyed her, chuckled a sexy sound that made the tiny hairs on the back of her neck rise, then slid his eyes to Harrison again.

"Sorry, man." His eyes met Marisol's. "*Harrison*, was just telling me that you two are an item. How long have you two been dating?"

She eyed Kincaid as firmly as he was eyeing her. His face was stone and his jaw muscles flexed. Was he angry, still? Or was he...jealous?

"Ah, not long," Harrison said, breaking the stupor

between them.

When she whipped her head toward Harrison, his pleading eyes wouldn't allow her to crush his fantasy in front of Kincaid. *Men and their egos.* She kneaded her earlobe, then stopped abruptly when she remembered what her aunt had told her about the action.

"Congratulations," Kincaid said. "Love is a beautiful thing."

As difficult as it was, she continued the charade. Folding her arms across her chest, she mumbled, "Thank you."

"Yes, thank you," Harrison said, pushing his chest out.

God, she felt sick. "You never said what you were doing here, Kincaid."

He hesitated a moment. "I heard your offer wasn't accepted on the bungalow. There's a property nearby I think you might like. I was headed that direction and thought I'd swing by to see if you wanted to check it out." He eyed Harrison. "That's if you don't mind, Henry."

"*Harrison,*" Marisol said, narrowing her eyes at Kincaid.

"My bad. I'm horrible with names."

That rang true, but she doubted it to be the reason for the lapse, especially after she'd witnessed a hint of a smirk on his face.

"Sounds good," Harrison said. "I'll be able to access the property for insurance purposes."

Kincaid flashed a look of pity and pointed over his shoulder. "Sorry, man. Had I known you would be here, I would have cleaned out my backseat. It's loaded with tools.

I'd put them in the bed, but it's full, too."

"Not a problem. I'll run home and get my vehicle. I need to change anyway. Jot down the address...*Kinnaird*, and *we'll* meet you there."

Kinnaird? Marisol shook her head. *Men*. Kincaid didn't appear the least bit thrilled by the mispronunciation of his name, but he'd started it. Nor did the suggestion of Harrison coming along seem to vibe with him. He glanced to her as if to encourage an intervention.

"Babe, it'll take me about fifteen minutes to get home. I'll pick you up shortly."

"Or she could just ride on your handlebars. That'll save you from having to drive all the way back over here," Kincaid said.

Marisol's eyes instinctively moved to the orange cruiser bike in the driveway. She hadn't ridden on the handlebars of a bicycle since she was much younger. With Kincaid. They'd had so much fun cycling around town. "*Cruising for love*," he used to say.

"You know what, Harrison... Why don't I just ride with Kincaid, and you join us? That'll give me some extra time to look around." And for her and Kincaid to finish where they'd left off.

Harrison flashed a frown, but didn't protest.

"Whatever you think is best, honey," he said.

Babe? Honey? She had to nip this in the bud. And soon.

"The address is—"

Harrison flashed his palm at Kincaid. "I'd better write this down. My memory is terrible." He pulled a pen and a

business card from his fanny pack and passed them to
Kincaid.

Kincaid jotted down the address and handed it back to
Harrison. Ha. He really did have a house to show her. For a
second, she thought it all could be a ruse.

"Well, I guess I'll see you two shortly." Harrison moved
to Marisol and kissed her on the cheek before strapping on
his helmet, mounting his bike and peddling away.

Kincaid snickered, but her eyes dared him to say one
word. He flashed his palms in mock surrender. This was
going to be a long ride.

The look on Kincaid's face—a gleam of victory—told
her he thought he'd won at whatever game he was playing.
"You ready to go?" he asked.

She experienced a moment of hesitation that passed
rather quickly. "Let me grab my purse and let Vaden know
I'm leaving. I'll meet you at your truck."

He nodded and strolled away.

Inside the house, she called out to Vaden. "Auntie?"

"Quit yelling, child, I'm right here."

Marisol glanced to her right. Vaden sat in the large
sitting room, a book flatten in her lap. Marisol glanced to
the open window that looked out onto the porch. "How
long have you been there?" she asked.

"Long enough to witness the trouble you're getting
yourself into."

"Kincaid just wants to show me a property I might be
interested in. It's strictly platonic."

"Not with the Tinsdale boy. The other one. The one
with the big ears. Something's off with that one. I don't like

him. Got them sneaky eyes."

Marisol laughed. "*Harrison*? Auntie, Harrison is as harmless as a mosquito."

Vaden grunted. "You think a mosquito is harmless, huh? Sit in a darkroom with one. Some men have a way of hiding their dark side."

Her aunt had a way of scaring the hell out of her with her blunt words.

"Don't play with his emotions, child," Vaden said.

The words made her cringe. "I won't," Marisol said. She kissed the top of Vaden's head, grabbed her purse and was off.

Kincaid waited by the passenger's side door of his truck. His eyes steadied on her, unnerving her more and more with every step she dared toward him. Was she really prepared to go another round? He broke eye contact long enough to open the door for her. When she slid into place, he reached over to assist with the seatbelt.

Her heart thumped when he draped his solid frame across her. His heat—powerful and intense—scorched her. She inhaled his manly scent—a mix of aftershave and cologne. *Mmm*. Being alone with him spoke volumes about her mental state. Coo-coo at best. Completely insane at worst.

To mask her growing anxiety and arousal, she said, "I can fasten my own seatbelt. I'm not an infant."

He flashed his palms. "Okay." After shutting her door, he jogged to the driver's side, taking his place behind the wheel.

Glancing over her shoulder, she said, "There's nothing

in your backseat."

Kincaid glimpsed into the backseat. "Huh. Would you look at that?" He shrugged. "Oops." The engine roared to life, and they were off.

Instead of tearing into Kincaid as she'd like to have done, Marisol decided to take a different approach. Yelling would accomplish nothing, evident by the fiasco on her aunt's porch. They were both adults, both capable of having an adult conversation.

Gathering her thoughts, she said, "Are you going to start the conversation about the other night, or am I?" Her head jerked forward when Kincaid came to a screeching halt in the middle of the road and forced the gear into park.

"A replaceable part in my life? Really, Marisol?"

When he snatched his red T-shirt over his head, exposing his lick-worthy chest, she gasped. The sight of his ripped abs caused her entire body to warm and tingle. Stimulation should have been the last thing she experienced, but it was an involuntary reaction.

"Does this look like a replaceable part?" He pointed to the tattoo that wrapped around his right bicep and spelled out PIXIE. Then to the tattoo over his heart that read MARISOL.

Pulling her eyes away, she trained them straight ahead. She didn't need a visual reminder. Kincaid replaced his shirt and moved to put the truck back into gear.

Marisol shifted toward him, staring him directly in the eyes. "When we broke up—"

His hand fell from the gear. "When you broke up with me," he said.

"Fine. When I broke up with you, I didn't think you would just give up. Love knows no limits. I thought you would travel to hell and back to make me yours again."

Kincaid's head fell back against the headrest. "I was in hell, Marisol. I traveled there the second you walked away. You went on with your life like we never existed, like *I* was the replaceable part."

The pain in his eyes ripped strands from her soul. She'd cried *poor me* for so long she never even considered that Kincaid had hurt, too. Her own broken heart had blinded her to the pieces of his. "I'm sorry. I played a childish game with your heart, with both of our hearts, and I lost."

"We both lost," he said, popping the truck into gear and giving it gas.

Marisol took his action as a signal that this was the end of the conversation. That was okay with her. She wasn't sure she could handle any more without bursting into tears.

"I came for you," Kincaid said, breaking the uncomfortable silence.

Marisol faced him again. "Came for me?"

"To Boston. A few months after you'd left. I searched the entire Harvard campus looking for you." He chuckled as if recalling a funny memory. "I'd never felt so out of place in my life. But I was determined to find you. To tell you how much I loved you. How I may not be everything you wanted, but that I could be everything you needed and more."

He'd always been everything she needed. "You came to Massachusetts?"

He nodded slowly. "You were in the library. You were

so gorgeous sitting at the table, your head buried in a book. So focused, so determined."

She'd spent most of her time in the library. Studying kept her mind off of him. In all honesty, he was responsible for every A she'd received.

Kincaid smoothed his hand down the side of his face. "I summoned all the courage I had lost standing there staring at you and moved toward the table, but…"

"What happened? What stopped you?"

He drummed his thumb against the steering wheel. "Carrot top."

"Carrot top?"

"The tall, lanky guy who joined you at the table. You seemed *really* happy to see him. You jumped up from your chair and draped your arms around his neck. It crushed me." His jaw flexed. "When you returned to your chair, you looked in my direction, as if you knew I was there. I darted out of sight."

"It was you. I thought my eyes were playing tricks on me, seeing what I wanted them to see. But you really were there. Why—?" The air in the cabin was so thick, it strangled her. "Why did you leave?"

"You'd clearly moved on. I figured I should, too. It wasn't that easy."

"No, Kincaid, I hadn't moved on. That was my study-buddy, Mark. He and his *boyfriend* had been attacked. The victims of a hate crime. I was so happy to see him because he'd been hospitalized for a month. He'd nearly died."

Kincaid eyed her. "You weren't seeing him?"

"No."

Kincaid cursed under his breath.

"Every day I fantasized about you coming to..." She paused and sighed. "How did we go so wrong, Kincaid?"

He massaged his temples. "I don't know. Can we just agree that we were young and dumb? That we were both at fault? And let the past go?"

Marisol nodded. "I would like that." What she would've liked more was to lean over and kiss him. Kiss him with the passion of a woman who hadn't kissed her lover in years.

Chapter 10

Kincaid felt as if a thousand pound weight he'd carried around for years had been lifted off his shoulders. Now that they'd gotten beyond the "easy" stuff—their past—it was time to face the hard—reclaiming Marisol's heart. His mind drifted to one major obstacle. *Harrison.* The thought of the man made his jaw clench.

By her silence, he knew their conversation still weighed heavy on her mind. Heck, his too. But they'd agreed to allow the past to remain there so there was no need to dredge up more of it. The way she rubbed the color off of her index finger with her thumb told him she was deep in thought about something.

He activated his turn signal and made a right onto Plum Lane. "You with me?" he asked.

Marisol pulled her gaze from the window. "All the way," she said.

Despite her lackluster tone, he liked the sound of *all the way*. All he wanted to do at this very second was slam his foot onto the brake, stretch his body across the cab of the truck and kiss Marisol until his lips were too raw and painful to continue. His self-control was quickly reaching its tipping point.

"Nice neighborhood, huh?" he asked, defusing the thought that had him aching to snatch her into his arms.

"Yes, it is. I don't remember it looking like this. The trees, a sidewalk. All of these gorgeous houses. Things certainly have changed."

Kincaid chuckled. Yes, they had. But he was referring more to them, than the neighborhood. Something felt different between them, less perplexing. Like a veil had been lifted and he was seeing things much clearer. The notion of winning Marisol back no longer seemed too farfetched. It actually felt more obtainable than ever.

"Please tell me that's the one," she said, pointing to a sage green bungalow with a standing FOR SALE sign in the yard.

Bringing his attention back to the reason they were there, he smiled. When they pulled into a driveway leading up to the house, Marisol squealed. Putting his truck into park, he relaxed against the seat. "So...what do you think?" he asked.

"What do I think?" She faced him. "I love it, Kincaid." Her eyes slid to his lips, but moved away fast. "I love it," she repeated, sliding her gaze back to the house.

"And Harrison..."

She whipped her head toward him, an expression of concern on her face. "What?"

"Do you think he'll approve?"

She released a shaky laugh. "Oh. I thought you were asking if I..." She waved her words off. "Never mind. It doesn't matter what Harrison thinks. He won't be living here with me."

"I'm sure he'll eventually want the two of you to live together. Don't you think?"

Marisol ignored him and gripped the door handle. "Let's go. I'm anxious to see the inside," she said, exiting the vehicle.

Hmm. Maybe Mason had been right about Marisol not being into the big-eared insurance man. He smirked and exited, too. As Marisol led the way to the house, Kincaid watched her hips sway from side-to-side in the khaki shorts she wore. The snug material accented her butt beautifully. A hunger stirred inside of him. How much longer could he resist holding her again, feeling her delicate body against him. He glanced heavenward. "Please give me strength," he mouthed.

"The door is locked," she said with a hint of disappointment in her tone.

"Then it's probably a good thing I have these," Kincaid said, dangling a set of keys at her.

She clapped and bounced her shoulders up and down like an excited toddler. "Yay."

After he'd unlocked the door and pushed it open, he stepped aside and allowed Marisol to enter first. The scent of her lotion, a blend of raspberry and vanilla, rushed up his nostrils as she inched by. He had a craving for something delicious, but not anything he would find on a menu.

"Would you look at this," Marisol said, taking in every inch.

The space wasn't expansive, but very appealing. It boasted an open floor plan with maple-colored hardwood floors that ran throughout the living area. Wainscoting and thick overhead wooden beams in the same maple hue gave the space character. Beyond the living space sat a small dining area separated by colonnades.

Kincaid followed Marisol through the space. "This kitchen…" she said, running her fingers over the stone island. "So much light. And all of this cabinet space." She eyed him. "How did you say you knew about this place?"

"I replaced the roof for the owner. He purchases properties, renovates them, then flips them for a profit.

"Ah. How many bedrooms does it have?"

"Two."

Kincaid led the way out of the kitchen and down the hall to the master bedroom. The first thing that seemed to catch her eye was the ceiling, where a Venetian ceiling fan hung from thin beams.

"Maple must have been the theme. It's everywhere, and I love it. I absolutely love it," Marisol said.

"The place is yours if you want it. I even got him to knock off a few thousand." Ten, to be exact. What he didn't tell her was that he would end up eating the cost in roofing work.

Marisol stared at him as if she was at a loss for words. A beat later, her lips spread into a toothy grin. "I want it. I want it," she repeated.

"I'll make the call," Kincaid said, excusing himself from the room.

"Kincaid, wait."

Marisol moved toward him, placing a warm hand on his forearm. Her touch sent a sensation through his body that settled below his waist. If this woman had any idea of the things he wanted to do to her, she wouldn't have been so close to him.

"Thank you for this. It means a lot to me that you...that we..." She sighed at her apparent inability to form her thought. "Thank you," she said, draping her arms around him.

The feel of her—soft and warm—against him caused a rumbled in his chest. He'd missed this, missed her, loved her like they'd never spent one day apart. Wicked, intense desire coursed through him as his need for her grew stronger and stronger until he couldn't contain it any longer.

He rested his hands on her hips and guided her away. What he witnessed in her eyes wasn't a surprise—confusion and longing. They wanted the same thing. Each other. She belonged to another and, under normal circumstances that would have meant something to him. But these weren't normal circumstances.

***

"What are we doing, Kincaid?" Marisol asked, groaning at the sensation that shot through her when he cupped her butt with both hands. His mouth dipped close to hers, his warm breath tickling her upper lip. He pecked her gently, then pulled away.

He said nothing. Not a single word to confirm what she already knew, despite asking the silly question. What he didn't say with his mouth, he conveyed with his body, pinning her against the wall. With one hand, he secured her arms above her head.

Marisol blew a long breath as his free hand crept slowly along her side, his eyes never leaving hers. The sensation caused her skin to prickle, nipples to harden, and the space between her legs to throb. Her breathing grew rapid and uncontrolled. A faint moan escaped when Kincaid's tongue glided across her bottom lip, then snaked inside her mouth.

"*Mmm*," she hummed.

The kiss was slow, gentle, and exploratory at first, as if giving her the opportunity to bring things to a halt. And if her brain had been working properly, maybe she would have.

The cautious kiss grew deeper, grew more passionate, grew more purposed. His tongue stroked hers as she greedily welcomed each thrust. His free hand rested on the back of her neck, pulling her mouth even closer to his. Every stroke of his tongue proved more gratifying than the last and delivered a mass of pleasure that had her pounding at the core.

After what seemed like an eternity, Kincaid pulled away, leaving her panting and wanting more. Much, much more. What she saw when she opened her eyes—passion, desire, a need for her on a level she'd never witnessed in any other man's eyes—warmed, thrilled, and frightened the hell out of her.

Maybe that fear—or self-preservation—caused her to say, "Harrison." A beat later, Kincaid ground his hardness against her. *Harrison, who?*

Kincaid held her face between his hands. "I don't think we have to worry about Harry. I may have given him the incorrect address. By accident, of course." He smirked. "Oops."

"Accident?" she said, absently. She took the initiative and pressed her lips to his. "Of course. Accident."

After another hungry kiss, Kincaid's mouth abandoned her lips again. He peppered kisses along her jawline and to her ear. "I want to make love to you, Marisol Chesapeake, like you couldn't imagine. I want to make you come until your body collapses into my arms."

She loved the way he said her full name during moments of heated passion. "Collapsing is good. Being in your arms, better."

He chuckled. "I plan to make love to you, like no man ever has." He kissed the tender space below her earlobe. "But not today."

"Wh…what? Not to—" Before she could finish the thought, he captured her protest with a kiss that could flatten hills. When the kiss ended, her knees wobbled.

"We'll make love, but not until I'm a hundred percent sure it's what you want. That I'm what you want."

Oh, God, she wanted it. Right now. Against what she hoped would be her bedroom wall. With trembling hands, she pulled at his zipper. "I want it. I want you. I've always wanted you." Something primal flashed in Kincaid's eyes, and the idea of what it meant set her on fire.

"I never could resist you," he said, hoisting her into his arms. "You'll always be my weakness. You'll always be my strength."

"You're the only—"

"*Hello?*"

Marisol froze, the air seizing in her lungs. "*Harrison?*" She flashed Kincaid a quizzical look before scrambling out of his arms and pushing him away. Straightening her clothing, she tossed him a narrow-eyed gaze. Had he lied to her about giving Harrison the wrong address? "Did you plan this? Did you want him to catch us?" she asked in a whisper.

Kincaid pulled his hands to his waist and stared at her, but remained silent.

Marisol rolled her eyes away. "In here, H...Harrison. The bedroom." She regretted the label the second the words escaped. When she discovered her beaded nipples peeping through her shirt, she folded her arms across her chest.

"There you are." Harrison smiled, adjusting his glasses. "I had one heck of a time finding you two. *Kinney*, I do believe you got your street names mixed up. You wrote *Pear* Lane. This is clearly *Plum* Lane."

Marisol felt horrible when she realized she'd falsely accused Kincaid. Her eyes slid to him briefly, meeting a face as tight as polished leather. Refocusing on Harrison, she said, "How'd you find us?" She hadn't meant for her words to sound so regretful.

"Well...I had to ride around looking for Kinney's truck." He removed his glasses, inspected them, then cleaned them with the hem of his shirt. "Sucks, too. Gas prices being what they are and all."

Was he serious? He drove an '89 Geo Metro. How much gas could it possibly take?

Harrison released a boisterous laugh. "Guess I'm not the only one with a shoddy memory, huh, *Kenly*?"

Alarm set in when Kincaid folded his arms across his chest, rocked back on his heels, and flashed a tight smile at Harrison. *County Fair*. This was the exact look Kincaid displayed right before he pounced on one of the Hollis twins for grabbing her butt. It'd taken three men to pull Kincaid off of him. It would take twice as many now.

Marisol swallowed hard as she ran her clammy hands over her shorts. *Say something*. "Ah...the kitchen. Let's take another look at the kitchen. It's amazing. Truly amazing." She urged Harrison toward the door.

As Harrison moved out of the room, Marisol turned to Kincaid and mouthed, "I'm sorry."

His body language—clenched jaw, a taut expression void of any emotion—told her it would take more than two words to smooth things over.

One thing was for sure... This house was not big enough for the three of them.

Chapter 11

Kincaid fumed the entire walk to the kitchen. These two could stroll around like a happy couple all they wanted, but he was out of there. And how could Marisol believe he wanted *Harry* to catch them having sex against the damn wall? Did she really believe he was capable of doing something like that? The Marisol he knew would have never thought so low of him. He didn't need this bullshit.

"I'm going to get out of here. Let you two lovebirds have some privacy," Kincaid said. By the look in Marisol's eyes, he'd touched a nerve. Good. "Lock the door on your way out." He hurried through the kitchen and out the front door.

Halfway to his truck, Harrison jogged up behind him. "Kincaid, hold up a minute."

Oh, so now the bastard wanted to get his name right. 'Course, he probably did deserve payback; he hadn't gone out of his way to get Harrison's name right. What in the hell did this lame want? Sighing, Kincaid turned to face him. As the man approached, he resisted the urge to knock him flat on his ass.

With a goofy smile on his face, Harrison said, "I just wanted to thank you for showing Marisol the house. She loves it. When my lady is happy, I'm happy."

Kincaid folded his arms across his chest and pinned his hands under his armpits to keep from swinging at this smug bastard. "Not a problem. You two enjoy." Kincaid turned and started away again.

"Ah, just one more thing," Harrison said.

Kincaid stopped mid-step. *Now what*?

"Stay away from her."

With his back still to Harrison, Kincaid drew his hands into tight balls. *Keep going. Just keep going.*

"You had your chance and blew it. Marisol's mine now."

Kincaid barked a humorless laugh. Over his shoulder, he said, "She's not a damn puppy." Taming the beast clawing to burst free, he forced his feet forward. "Nice chatting with you, *Holloman*."

"*Harrison, motherf...*" His words trailed off, probably remembering he was supposed to be the good guy.

Behind the wheel of his truck, Kincaid shot a not-so-cordial glare in Harrison's direction, then slid it to the porch where Marisol stood, her arms cradling her body. Even from where he sat, he saw the tenderness in her eyes. Why couldn't he stop loving that woman?

With a flick of the wrist, his truck roared to life. Yanking the shift into gear, he peeled out of the driveway, leaving a cloud of white smoke trailing behind him. This wasn't how he'd imagined the day would go.

Kincaid gave himself an imaginary pat on the back. It'd taken a whole lot of restraint to not wrap his hands around Harry's scrawny neck and squeeze. He wasn't so confident that the next time their paths crossed he would be so lenient. Especially if he tried to flex his muscle and command him to stay away from Marisol again.

"*Stay away from her*." Kincaid laughed at the man's warning. Who in the hell did he think he was? He'd see

Marisol any damn time he wanted to see her. Harry's dumbass certainly wouldn't stop him.

Recalling the overly confident expression on Harrison's face when he called Marisol his lady, Kincaid struck the steering wheel. "Damn," he said, shaking off the sharp pain that shot up his arm. But the memory of Marisol's soft, sweet lips against his replaced the discomfort with a feeling of euphoria. He smirked. *A couple of minutes more and ole Harry boy would've gotten an eyeful. Damn bloodhound.*

A hint of Marisol's scent still lingered on his T-shirt, and he lifted the fabric to his nose. "Stay away from her," he said out loud. "In your dreams, *Harry*." They'd started something inside the bedroom that needed to be finished. "One way or the other," he mumbled.

A few hours later, Kincaid pulled into his driveway. When he entered the house, he headed straight for his workout room. A little sweat therapy was just what he needed to take his mind off of Marisol, Harrison, the entire horrid mess. Stripping out of his T-shirt, he positioned himself on the weight bench and gripped the chilled metal bar.

"Stay away from her." Why couldn't he force the warning from his thoughts? The adrenaline surging through him resulted in a boost of energy that he took full advantage of, lifting rigorously. Who the hell did he think he was giving orders?

When he couldn't lift anymore, he returned the bar to its proper position and sat forward. Using his shirt, he wiped away the lines of sweat running down his face and chest, then studied the tattoo scribed over his heart. Was he wasting his time?

The doorbell sounded, redirecting his attention. He glanced at the wall clock. *Seven thirty*. "They're early," he said, referring to the friends he was expecting, but not for another hour. He tossed his drenched shirt over the bar and headed for the door.

"You're early," he said, yanking open the door. "*Oh...* It's you."

Marisol darted past him. "Love—" She stopped abruptly, her eyes sliding to his bare chest. "—birds?" Finding his eyes again, she said, "You are unbelievable."

A part of him wanted to toss her out on her ass, but another part—the more consuming part—was happy she'd come. "That's what you two are, right? Lovebirds? Lovers?" He eased the door closed.

"What kind of woman do you think I am, Kincaid? If—"

"What kind of man do you think I am, Marisol? Do you really think I would plan for your *lover* to walk in on us making love? I had no idea you were dating a damn bloodhound."

Marisol rested her hand on the side of her neck. In a calm tone, she said, "If Harrison and I were *lovers*, would I have kissed you like...like..."

"Like this?" he said, snatching her into his arms and smashing his lips to hers. She resisted at first, but slowly melted in his arms. Her moans alerted him to her satisfaction. That seductive sound was music to his ears. It didn't take much for his body to respond to their connection. When he pulled away, Marisol had a goofy look on her face. "Like that?" he asked, with a grin.

"Yeah," she said breathlessly. "Just like that." The second her eyes popped open, the satisfied expression on her face dissolved into one of fear and confusion. She planted her hands onto his chest and pushed him away. "I...I have to go," she mumbled and brushed past him.

Kincaid released a tortured grunt. In an elevated tone, he said, "What do you want, Marisol?" When she didn't answer, through clenched teeth, he said, "What, Marisol?"

Over her shoulder, she said, "You, Kincaid. I want you. I've always wanted you." Her hand gripped the doorknob, but she didn't turn it.

Kincaid moved behind her, hooked his arm around her waist and pulled her to him. With her back resting against his chest, he kissed the back of her head. "Then why are you running from me? Talk to me."

"I'm so confused." Her tone grew delicate and low. "If I don't run from you, I'll run to you."

"And what's so wrong with that?"

"I'm not sure I'm ready. I'm afraid."

His hands slid to her hips and he rotated her to face him. "Afraid of what?"

She glanced up at him with tear-filled eyes. "Being hurt. Being disappointed."

"You have to know I would never hurt you." Paige's name popped into his head. "Not intentionally. When I told you I would love you until the end of time, I meant it. I've never stopped loving you, Marisol. In ten years, I've never spent one single day without you in my heart. You ruined me. I don't think I could love another woman if I tried. Not like a man is supposed to love his woman. That kind of love has and always will be reserved for only you."

A tear trailed down her cheek. "I..." She swallowed hard.

Kincaid held her face between his hands. "Do you still love me?"

Marisol's lips parted, but before she could supply an answer, the doorbell rang.

"*Shit*," Kincaid said. "Give me two seconds. I'll tell the guys I can't make it tonight."

"No," Marisol said. "We'll talk later. You have plans. Please don't alter them for me." She rested a warm hand on the side of his face. "We'll talk tomorrow."

A beat later, she opened the door and darted past Hoyt and Logan—two of his childhood friends.

"Damn, Tinsdale. You still making the girls cry," Logan said.

Kincaid ignored the man and hurried after Marisol. She wasn't going to get away that easily. "Marisol, wait." Despite his plea, she kept moving. Blocking her entrance into the vehicle, he placed his hand under her chin and forced her to look at him. "Do you still love me?"

Marisol snatched away. "I'm not the fifteen-year-old you fell in love with years ago, Kincaid. I'm not the same woman you once knew."

"Do you still love the sound of rain hitting against the window? Candlelit baths? Thin crust pepperoni pizza with extra cheese? Sandpaper rough toilet tissue?"

This garnered a faint smile from Marisol. "It makes me feel cleaner," she said.

"I know you, Marisol. And what I don't know, I want to

learn."

Marisol studied him. "After everything I've put you through...you still love me, still want to be with me?"

"That was the past, remember? We're done with that phase. The only thing that matters is the present and the future. *Our* future. Together."

She sneered. "You make it sound so simple."

"Simple is what we make it. This is what we make it. I love you. And I know you still love me, too. Even if you don't want to admit it. But that's okay..." He brushed a bent finger across her cheek. "...because I want you to forget you love me."

She chuckled. "At this point, I don't think that's possible. But out of curiosity, why?"

He rested a hand on either side of her neck and pulled her face close to his. "Because I want to make you fall in love with me all over again."

Her lips parted, but he tilted his head forward and kissed her before any words escaped. Kissed her in a way that he hoped convinced her of the possibilities. Kissed her in a way that revealed his sincerity. Kissed her in a way that told her he was hers and only hers.

When he pulled away, Marisol's eyes sparkled. She ran her thumb across his bottom lip. Capturing her hand, he kissed the tips of her fingers one by one.

"That's so beautiful," came from the porch, but his focus remained pinned to Marisol.

"Trust me," he said. "Love is all we need."

Marisol nodded, but by the expression on her face, he wasn't sure she was convinced.

Chapter 12

Marisol dragged into the kitchen to see Vaden punching down a batch of dough. Judging by the amount of cakes, pies, and pans on the stove, she'd been at it since the crack of dawn. That was Vaden. Up with the roosters.

Marisol shook her head. Did the woman ever take a break? If she wasn't hustling and bustling around the diner, attending a church function, or volunteering for a community event, she was cooking a feast for her and her brothers as she was doing now and every Sunday.

Vaden had the energy of a woman ten times her junior, and Marisol could use a dose, because her conversation with Kincaid the evening before still had her drained. And confused. She couldn't forget confused.

"Morning," Marisol said, taking a whiff of the aromas swirling around the room. "It smells good in here."

"Well, good morning." Using the hem of her apron, Vaden dried her hands. "There's coffee on the stove."

"Great. I need it."

Vaden was the only person she knew who still used an old school coffee percolator instead of a machine. But this aged device made one heck of a cup of coffee. Nothing like the watered down crap she was used to. After filling her cup, she rested against the counter and savored the strong brew. "Mmm," that's so good."

"I kept your plate warm. It's in the oven. You have to be starving. You barely touched your plate last night at dinner."

"I didn't have much of an appetite."

"Got anything to do with that Tinsdale boy? And by the way, you tell him I'm still waiting for him to replace my petunias." Vaden shook her head. "Lord, that boy's got feet the size of a rowboat. Squashed half of my babies."

Anything to do with that Tinsdale boy? Seems like since she'd returned to Indigo Falls, everything had to do with that Tinsdale boy. Her thoughts, her dreams. Marisol eyed the steam rising from her mug. "He told me he loved me," she said.

"I see. And do you believe him?"

Marisol's eyes rose to meet her aunt's. "Yes, I do. Am I crazy?"

Vaden chuckled. "Yes, you are, child. And it's called being in love. Love will make you crazy as a bedbug." Vaden turned back to the counter and started peeling potatoes. "And I'm assuming you handled that other problem."

"Yes, ma'am, I did. And you were right about Harrison having a dark side."

Marisol's thoughts drifted to the car ride back home with Harrison. Along the route, she'd given him the "*It's not you, it's me*" line. Along with the "*You'll make someone a great guy*" line. Then wrapped it all up neatly with "*I hope we can still be friends.*"

At one point, she thought he'd pull the car over and put her out on the side of the road. Then the conversation shifted to the gas he'd wasted gallivanting—as he'd put it—around town. Feeling guilty, she'd given him fifty dollars—far more than the putt-putt he drove could hold.

Coasting back to reality, Marisol said, "His dark side is

greed."

"I'm not surprised. I've heard about those ridiculous prices he charges for insurance. Somebody needs to report him."

Marisol placed her mug down. "On a happier note, I absolutely loved the house. It's perfect. I'll hopefully be out of your hair soon. Aren't you glad?"

"No, child. I'm going to miss you when you're gone. You know you don't have to leave. You can stay here as long as you want. I enjoy the company. It gets lonely in this big ole house alone.

"Auntie?" she said, grabbing one of the green beans on the counter. "Can I ask you something?"

"I reckon so."

"Why didn't you ever re-marry?" Marisol remembered how men fell at Vaden's feet, but she never gave any of them the time of day.

The peeler briefly stilled in Vaden's hand. "Once was enough for me."

"Weren't you happy?"

Without skipping a beat, she said, "No, I wasn't. I wasn't happy because I wasn't in love with my husband."

With furrowed brow, Marisol shifted toward her aunt. "Why did you marry someone you didn't love?"

Vaden stared aimlessly out of the window. "The man I truly loved, the man I should have married, wasn't prominent enough in your grandfather's eyes. He didn't come from money. Didn't have a name like Chesapeake. Unlike Lendell, whose family was well-known and had clout. That never appealed to me, but it sure did to your grandfather."

Marisol's heart broke for Vaden. She couldn't imagine marrying a man she didn't love, which was why she'd said no to Patrick every time he'd popped the question. "Did you tell grandfather you loved another man?"

Vaden laughed softly. "A janitor's son wasn't good enough for his only daughter. That's what he said to me." She shook her head. "Your grandfather was a good man, Pixie, but power and prestige meant more to him than true love ever could."

"Couldn't you have stood up to him? Fought for the man you loved and refused to marry a man you didn't?"

"I did." Vaden wiped her hands down the front of her apron. "Daddy threatened to bankrupt his family if I didn't go through with the marriage. I couldn't allow that to happen."

Marisol didn't say it aloud, but her grandfather sounded like a monster. "You made the ultimate sacrifice for the man you loved."

Vaden frowned. "I guess you could say that."

"My mother didn't come from money. Why did grandfather approve of my father marrying her?"

"Because your father didn't give him a choice. Nothing meant more to your father than your mother. And daddy knew that. Daddy knew that if he didn't accept your mother, he'd lose his only son. If that happened, who would carry on the Chesapeake legacy?"

"Did grandfather like my mother?" Marisol said, afraid of the answer.

"Your mother was as pretty as a porcelain doll with a

heart like gold. Just like you. She stole Daddy's heart, and he loved her like a second daughter."

The information made Marisol smile and helped to redeem the man she'd never known. She thought about the statue of her grandfather that sat in the town square. She'd heard stories of how great he was, but she got the impression that people feared him more than liked him.

"I thought I could learn to love Lendell."

Wow. That was the same thing she'd told herself about Patrick. It hadn't worked for her, but maybe it had for Vaden.

"Only thing I learned was love don't work that way." Vaden's face contorted into a tight ball, and she stared off again as if she were recalling something awful. "I loathed him with every fiber of my being. Once we took vows, he became a cold, cruel man."

Marisol understood cold and cruel. When Patrick drank too much—as he often did—he become someone she barely recognized. And like Vaden, she'd grown to hate him.

"*Damn*."

Marisol's attention snapped back to Vaden. "Oh, no. You've cut yourself." Snatching a dishtowel, she wrapped it around her aunt's bleeding finger. "Let me get you cleaned up."

"Child, don't fuss over me. It's just a paper cut. A little flour and I'll be as good as new."

"Come on, young lady." Marisol directed her to the table, then collected the first-aid kit. As she cleaned and bandaged her aunt's finger, Marisol said, "It's the age of technology, Auntie. Have you thought about Googling your first love?"

Vaden swatted her away. "That's enough fussing." She pushed to her feet and moved back to the sink. "I've got plenty left to do. And your brothers will be here any minute. Did I tell you Janelle Washington purchased the old doughnut shop?"

Marisol laughed to herself at her aunt's apparent attempt at deflecting the conversation.

"It's going to be a custom cakery. Whatever that is. Laz is helping her renovate it. I sure do like her. Maybe your brother will get some good sense about him and ask her out instead of—"

"It's Baxter, isn't it?"

Vaden busied herself. "What about Baxter, child?"

"He's your first love."

Vaden went stiff as a board. Starting to stir again, she said, "What makes you say something crazy like that?"

"I see the affectionate way he looks at you. The way you two look at each other at the diner. With respect, admiration." Marisol joined her at the sink. "Love. Pure and true."

Vaden made wide circle on the counter with the rag. "You've always been too observant."

"Does that mean I'm right?"

Vaden chuckled. "Yeah, you're right. I hurt that man. When I told him I was marrying Lendell, it tore him to pieces. It was the hardest thing I'd ever had to do. I've never forgiven myself."

Marisol wrapped her arms around Vaden. So much of what Vaden said, she could relate to. "Oh, Auntie. I'm so sorry."

"Wasn't your fault, child. Ain't no need for you to apologize." Vaden patted Marisol's arms. "He said he understood. Whether that was true or not, I don't know. He never asked why. And despite what I was doing to him, he looked me square in the eyes and told me he would love me and me alone until the day he died."

Marisol thought about the conversation she and Kincaid had had the evening before. He'd said something similar to her. "Losing each other had to be devastating for you both." She could definitely relate to that pain.

"It was. I'd sacrificed a kind, gentle man for a scathing beast that used me as a punching bag whenever he saw fit. And he always saw fit," she said, a hint of anger in her voice.

Marisol gasped. "He...hit you?" Her words were cautious and filled with disbelief.

Vaden nodded slowly.

"What did... How... Why did you stay?"

"That's what women did back in those days. We suffered, but we never split up our family."

"Did grandfather know?"

"No one knew about the silent hell I was living in. Not even your mother, who was my very best friend in this world."

A thousand question raced through Marisol's head. "Why didn't you tell my father? You said the two of you were close."

"Child, your father would have killed Lendell dead as dirt if I'd told him. I couldn't allow him to risk his family for me. Galen was a toddler and your mother was pregnant with Colton."

Listening to Vaden's story was like glancing into the mirror at her own life. The hurt, the pain, the sorrow. "Did it get better?"

"Not even after I got pregnant."

"*Pregnant*?" Marisol said gently. Vaden didn't have children. That had to mean... *Oh, God. She'd lost the baby.* An overwhelming sadness settled over Marisol, because she knew Vaden would have been a great mother. She had been to her and her brothers.

"One day I put too much corn in the vegetable soup. Lendell went ballistic. Beat me like I was a man. I was three months gone then. He tossed me around like I was nothing more than a ragdoll."

"Auntie, you don't have to talk about this."

Vaden smiled. "It feels good to finally get it all out. Sometimes you just have to talk about things to make them better."

Staring into her aunt's eyes, Marisol recognized the still fresh wounds.

"One night Lendell fell into a drunken stupor. When he did, I ran. Ran until my legs couldn't take me any further. I must have collapsed, because when I woke, I was in Baxter's strong arms." Vaden's face glowed as if recalling the moment gave her life.

Marisol perked up with surprise. "Baxter?"

"He looked down into my bruised and battered face and said, '*He'll never hurt you again, my sweet Vaden flower.*'" Vaden's face brightened again with the recalled sentiment. "He cleaned the blood from body, nursed me

110

back to health. I fell in love with that man all over again. His love healed me. But as bad as I wanted to, I couldn't stay there."

"Why?" Marisol asked, holding tight to Vaden's every word.

"My being there put him in danger. It was only a matter of time before Lendell found me. And if he found me with Baxter, he would have killed us both."

"Did Lendell come looking for you?"

"Yes, but he never found me. Baxter was determined to keep me safe. I was prepared to leave everything behind, including my family, to get away from Lendell. But, I didn't have to. They found Lendell's body in the hay barn, a shotgun stuffed in his mouth."

Marisol slapped her hand over her mouth. A beat later she allowed it to fall. "Did Baxter—"

Vaden flashed her palm. "Don't ask that question, child. For forty years, I've allowed myself to believe Lendell loved me so much he couldn't bear living without me. As far as I'm concerned, he took his own life. The doctor agreed."

Marisol wanted to ask a thousand more questions, but she honored Vaden's wishes. "Why did you not marry Baxter? You were free."

Vaden's eyes slid toward the refrigerator. "In a way, Lendell still has a hold on me."

Marisol followed Vaden's gaze to the vintage Maxwell House coffee can. Now she knew why Vaden hadn't bothered to purchase an elegant urn. Instead, she'd had Lendell's ashes stored in the rusty tin. Marisol shivered at the thought that she'd almost brewed a cup of him when she was younger. Drinking him would have been too good for a monster like him.

Vaden released a soft chuckle. "Besides, Baxter never asked me to marry him."

If Marisol knew anything about her aunt, it was the woman never told a story without cause. Telling this account of her life wasn't by coincidence. "You know, don't you?" Marisol said, refusing to look at the woman.

"I suspected."

"H…" Marisol swallowed hard. "How?"

"When you first arrived, you flinched when I put my arms around you. That told me the last arms you were in weren't so gentle."

"Like you, I stayed for all of the wrong reasons. I was there because of what I thought he could do for my career. I thought that maybe, just maybe I'd learn to love him." Marisol balled her hands into tight fists. "I was so foolish to stay."

With stern words, Vaden held her at arm's length and said, "Child, you got out. That's all that matters. You got out of that toxic relationship."

"There was a young woman…" Marisol paused, gathering the strength she needed to continue. "A young woman not much older than me. Bruises, lacerations, broken bones. Her husband had beaten her to death. Her own husband, Auntie. What kind of monster does that to the woman he's supposed to love?"

"Unfortunately, it happens every day. Every damn day."

"I stared at her for what seemed like hours. There on

112

my autopsy table, her blonde hair streaked with crimson, eyes swollen to the size of golf balls, flesh torn and black and blue. I stared down into her face..." Marisol flashed back to the moment and tears streamed down her cheeks. "I stared down into her face, and I saw myself lying there. My once warm body sprawled out on that cold metal table. I knew it was only a matter of time before his shoving and pushing escalated to punches. I didn't want to end up like Brittany Vincent." The young woman's name was stuck in her head.

"You're here now, child. Safe and sound in Indigo Falls. Nothing or nobody will hurt you here. I swear that on my life."

"I ran, too, Auntie. I ran until I was in the only place I could feel safe. Until I was with the only people I knew would never hurt me. And I'm still running. I want to stop, but I can't. I'm still running. From life, from love, from Kincaid. He wants to love me, but I'm too afraid to let him. Too afraid of taking that chance. What do I do, Auntie?" She shook her head. "What do I do?"

Vaden eyed her sternly. "Don't make the same mistake I did. That Tinsdale boy is your Baxter. You let him love you. Let that man love you so hard that you forget why you don't think you deserve it. The healing power of love is amazing. Let it mend you."

"I feel so lost, so confused."

"If you're not ready, don't rush or force it. If he's serious about loving you, he'll wait until you're able to give him what he needs."

Marisol couldn't help but wonder for how long, or if he

would wait at all. More importantly, was it fair to ask him to.

***

Kincaid sat in his truck on the street outside Vaden's house, dreading to climb the stairs and ring the doorbell. If he'd had his way, he'd have simply mailed her a check for the flowers he'd destroyed. But she had sent word that if he didn't replace the petunias he'd trampled, she'd ring his neck. He was certain it wasn't an idle threat. All of the elders in Indigo Falls were built Ford tough. Vaden was no exception. If he didn't know any better, he'd swear the woman hated him.

He'd expected to see Marisol's car parked in the driveway when he arrived—especially since when they'd spoken earlier in the day, she'd said she had something important to talk to him about. Then he'd remembered today was one of the days she volunteered at the clinic. God, he loved that woman and her big heart.

Instead of prolonging the inevitable, he slinked out of his truck. What was the big deal? He would only have to be there ten minutes, fifteen tops. Just long enough to unload the bed full of flowers.

At the Perfect Posey Garden and Nursery, Kincaid had to endure Mr. Conley's drawn out lecture when he'd asked what was the most popular petunia color. Tiring of listening to the man's slow country drawl, he purchased twenty containers of each color he had in stock. Purples, pinks, reds, whites, striped and so on.

Vaden was already eyeing him through the screen door by the time he made it onto the porch. The woman made him far more nervous than any father could. *In and out*, he reminded himself.

"Afternoon, Ms. Vaden," he said, removing the black ball cap he'd been wearing with Tinsdale Roofing stitched across the front in white lettering. "I have the petunias you wanted." He pointed over his shoulder. "They're in my truck. Where would you like them?"

"In the ground. You can start planting them exactly where you trampled my other ones," she said, not a hint of a smile on her face.

Did she just say start planting them? Kincaid rubbed the side of his face. With a shaky smile, he said, "You want *me* to plant them?"

Vaden placed her hands on her hips. "Who did you think would plant 'em?"

Kincaid didn't dare say, "You," despite the word dancing on the tip of his tongue. He didn't know shit about gardening, but hey, any fool could dig a hole and drop a flower in, right?

"No problem. Guess I should get started."

After only twenty minutes, Kincaid was ready to end his own life. No need. Ten more minutes and the heat would do it for him. The temperature was a hundred degrees pass hell, and the sun beat down on him like a vengeful god. Sweat spilled from every pore, his skin burned and he was sure he was about to collapse from heatstroke. He didn't even require his men to be out in temperatures this blistering. It had to be at least ninety.

"You look a little thirsty," Vaden said, nearing him with a tray holding a pitcher of lemonade and two glasses. "Lord, it sure is hot out here. The devil would need air conditioning today. You should've waited for a day that wasn't so dang hot to plant all of these flowers. But you're doing a good job."

"Thank you." He didn't say too much, just in case she got the wrong idea that he liked gardening. Vaden placed the tray on a small patio table, filled a glass, and passed it to him. He emptied the liquid in three large gulps.

"I guess you were thirsty." She settled in a green Adirondack chair worn by time.

Kincaid had to admit he'd been far more comfortable when Vaden had simply watched him from the comforts of the kitchen window. If he'd known he'd wind up planting these stupid petunias, he would have never purchased so many. He hated them. Hated, hated, hated petunias.

"You like petunias?" Vaden asked.

Kincaid straightened and ran the back of his dirt-covered hand across his brow. *Hell, no.* "I'm not much of a flower person."

"You see those petunias right there." She pointed to a patch of white and purple flowers to her right. "I got those free at Booker's Furniture. They'd bought a whole mess of 'em to give away as a promotion. They were going to toss the leftovers out."

He wasn't sure what to say. "They look...*healthy*."

Vaden smiled for the first time since he'd arrived. "They are now. When I first got 'em, they looked horrible. Wilted and starving for water. Brown petals. Just plain battered," she said with a look of contempt.

Clearly, she took gardening serious.

"Sometimes it's hard to tell what's going on inside of flowers, just like with people. But I knew those petunias were still full of life. They just needed a reason to grow. I brought 'em home, planted 'em, watered 'em, even talked to 'em every now and then."

Kincaid's brows furrowed, but he didn't reveal what was on his mind. Which was, "You talked to petunias?"

"All they needed was a little TLC. They just needed to be assured that it was okay for them to bloom. They needed encouragement. And that's exactly what I gave 'em." She beamed. "Now just look at 'em. Thriving."

Vaden's brown eyes settled on him and something in her demeanor shifted.

"A flower can't always tell you what's stunting its growth. Sometimes it simply requires nurturing. Pixie used to love gardening." Vaden shifted her eyes back to the flowers. "On the outside, those flowers are radiant, appear to be full of life. But on the inside, they need TLC. A lot of cultivating. Those beauties have been through a lot."

Something about the cryptic way she spoke told Kincaid they were no longer talking about petunias. This caused his curiosity to run amok. If they were in fact now talking about Marisol, what had she gone through? The thought of her experiencing anything awful unnerved him.

Vaden's eyes settled sternly on him. "You have to be patient with something as delicate as a petunia. Especially when it wants to bloom, but not sure if it should risk showing its blossoms." She paused a moment, then added,

117

"It's amazing what love can do...*for petunias*."

Yes, he was receiving her message loud and clear.

"The thing with gardening, son, is you can't give up simply because the blooms are a bit stubborn."

He laughed and so did Vaden.

"If you want them to reveal what lies beneath their protective bud, you have to keep giving them what they need. Which is love. Lots and lots of love. Then, one day when you least expect it, they open up and reveal all of their hidden beauty to you."

Kincaid nodded slowly, signaling he understood every word.

"Whelp, I've lollygagged long enough. I have plenty of housework to do. I'll leave you to your gardening." She pushed to her feet and strolled away.

"Ms. Vaden," Kincaid called out. When she turned to face him, he said, "I love petunias."

She cracked a smile. "Son, I have absolutely no doubt you do. Who else plants them in thousand degree temperatures?" She winked and continued into the house.

Suddenly, it didn't feel so hot anymore.

Chapter 13

Marisol stood at Kincaid's front door trying to conger the courage to ring the bell. It would serve her right if he opened the door, then slammed it in her face. For the past two days, she'd alienated him without the least hint of an explanation as to why. Hell, she didn't even know why herself. All she knew was somewhere between standing in his driveway a few nights ago and pouring her heart out to Vaden, something had changed, causing her to tuck tail and run.

No more running.

Snatching in a deep breath, she released it slowly and lifted her hand, but before she could press the bell, the door eased open and like magic, Kincaid appeared. Marisol swallowed hard and took in all of him filling the threshold. The red polo shirt and red and white chessboard shorts he wore looked great on him, plus accented his chocolate tone.

Kincaid didn't appear as stunned by her presence as she was of his. He'd caught her off guard. She could have used those extra seconds to sooth her rattled nerves. But here he was, fine and tempting as ever.

"Marisol?" he said dryly, then leaned against the doorjamb and folded his arms across his chest. He glanced past her as if she wasn't standing there. "I'm surprised to see you."

His tone was cold and held no enthusiasm, but she understood why. "You should be upset with me. I…" She closed her eyes briefly to get her thoughts together.

Opening them again, she settled back on him. "I'm a coward."

The words seemed to garner his undivided attention and his firm demeanor softened. Pushing away from the doorjamb, he stood upright, his arms falling to his sides. His brows furrowed, but relaxed just as quickly. "Meaning?"

"For the past two days, I've been trying to figure out a way to tell you this wouldn't work, that *we* wouldn't work." Kincaid started to speak, but Marisol paused him with a flash of her palm. "Please, I need to say this."

Kincaid obliged, but not without obvious regret. He folded his arms across his chest again and shrugged a shoulder. "Okay."

She wrung her hands together as she spoke. "What I want... What I'm trying to say..." Marisol paused and cradled herself in her arms, lowering her eyes a second time. "Whew, this is harder than I imagined."

Kincaid—clearly exhausted by her start-stop way of communicating—placed a finger under her chin and lifted her head. "Just say it, Marisol. Whatever it is, just say."

Lost in his kind eyes and comforting tone, Marisol said, "I didn't believe love was enough. I was wrong. You're my Baxter."

Kincaid's brows arched, and a quizzical expression spread across his face.

"I can't tell you what that means, at least not right now, but it's a very, very good thing. I love you, Kincaid Tinsdale. I'm scared as hell of getting this thing wrong again, but... I love you and don't want to wake up one day and wonder, what if? I don't want to regret the chance I was too afraid to take. Maybe I don't even deserve you, Kincaid, but I want you in my life."

After saying the words, Marisol wasn't sure what she expected from Kincaid. What she received—as simple as it was—pleasantly surprised her. A hug. One that swallowed her whole. Gentle. Encompassing. Protective. Familiar. His embrace captivated her in a manner that not even the most passionate of kisses could have. It all became clear why no other man's arms had ever been able to completely comfort her.

Loving him made her vulnerable, exposed her to unimaginable hurt, inconceivable pain. But the fear from the notion faded the second Kincaid pulled away and stared into her eyes.

"This is a little bitter-sweet," he said.

A hint of alarm settled inside her. Had he decided she wasn't worth the trouble? The thought tore at her like a dull knife. "Why?" she asked, unsure if she was prepared for the answer.

"Because I was sure you were trying to walk away from me, from us. This time, baby, I was prepared to fight like hell for you. What am I going to do with all of this energy now?"

She wanted to provide a few suggestions, but resisted. Sex would come, and as much as she desired—no craved—him, taking things slow had to be their approach. She hoped he could understand.

As if he'd read her mind, he cradled her face between his hands and said, "We'll take things as slow as we need to take them. I don't want to rush. I just want to love you."

Marisol's eyes clouded with tears. She couldn't find the words to express how much what he'd just said meant to her. Moving her mouth to his, she kissed him in a manner that spoke volumes, allowing passion do the talking for her.

Shaky hands rippled over his muscles as she stroked them up and down his arms. The feel of his solid frame caused her body to respond the way it always did when she lingered this close to that Tinsdale boy. A gush of something warm and soothing flooded her. When Kincaid's mouth left hers, the need to taste him, to have him inside of her was overwhelming.

"Slow," he said.

Marisol wasn't sure if he was trying to convince himself or her, but judging by the bulge pressing against her, she wasn't the only one experiencing a sexually charged moment. She wanted to yell, "*To hell with slow.*" Long, hard, and fast was how she wanted it. In the kitchen, on the floor, against the wall... It didn't matter. She just wanted it. Calming her hypersensitive libido, she nodded. "Slow."

***

Marisol placed a yellow bandage with Daffy Duck printed on it across little Crystal Meyer's leg. She'd fallen off of her bicycle and scratched her knee. Her father, Roman, had rushed her into the clinic, suggesting she needed an X-ray, MRI, CT scan, and a list of a hundred other unnecessary tests. After convincing him that Crystal hadn't broken any bones—or suffered any internal injuries—he'd settled down.

Although a bit overprotective, in her opinion, she admired the fact that he seemed to regard his job as a father with the utmost importance. He was new to Indigo Falls. In passing, she'd heard he'd lost his wife a year earlier to cervical cancer. Crystal had clearly become the center of his universe.

"You are all set, pretty girl," Marisol said, pushing from her knelt position in front of Crystal. "As good as new."

"Thank you so much, Dr. Chesapeake. When she fell, she hit the ground so hard I was sure she'd broken something," Roman said.

"I didn't even cry when I fell off my big girl bike, did I, Daddy?" Crystal said, her mouth purple from the grape lollipop one of the nurses had given her prior to coming back to the examining room.

"No, baby, you didn't. Daddy is the one who did all of the crying." He flashed an expression that was a mix between embarrassment and shame.

"You did what most fathers would have done. Besides, I much prefer you brought her in and there be no problem, than you not bring her and there'd been a serious one."

He nodded as if that had been his reasoning. "You're good at this. Do you have kids?"

"Thank you. And no, I don't have kids." Not yet, at least. But she wanted them. A house full. Coming from a large family, she couldn't imagine not having at least six kids, which meant she'd have to have them back-to-back. She wasn't getting any younger. The thought of babies made her smile.

"That's a shame. Something tells me you would be a great mother."

She hoped she would be at least half the mother Vaden had been to her. Even at half, that would mean she was phenomenal.

Roman smiled revealing a set of the whitest teeth she'd ever seen. She hadn't paid much attention before—with his panicked behavior and constant glancing over her shoulder—but Roman Meyers was quite the looker. Not as handsome as her Kincaid, but he could certainly turn a head or two.

Tall, smooth caramel-colored skin, broad shoulders... A thought snaked into her head. More like a name...*Rayah*. They would make a beautiful couple. And Rayah absolutely adored children. Heck, she owned a daycare center. What screamed "I love kids" more than that?

Marisol smiled to herself and at Roman, but for two totally separate reasons. How fun would it be to double date like she and Rayah had done years ago. "So, Mr. Meyer, how do you like it here in Indigo Falls?"

He folded one arm across his chest and nodded. "It's growing on me. Everyone is so friendly. It's a huge difference living here than it was living in Durham. The noise, the crime, the violence. We didn't live in the best part." He shrugged. "But my wife loved it there, so we stayed for her."

"You'll love it here," she said. "Does Crystal attend Sugar Plums Daycare?"

"No. I work from home, so it's not necessary to utilize the afterschool program there. Although, I hear it's great. A number of my clients have kids enrolled there."

"It is. My best friend Rayah owns and operates it. She's fantastic with kids."

"Rayah? She's Merle B's daughter, right?"

Uh-oh. With the mention of Merle B's name, things were destined to go downhill from there. Merle B was like Rayah's scarlet letter. It'd been that why since they were young. Men just assumed Rayah was just as headstrong as her mother could be. "Yes, she is."

Roman's expression turned serious. "Merle B... She was great to us when we first moved here. If it wasn't for her, I'd still be trying to get my utilities turned on." He massaged his chin. "She's good people." Shifting his attention to Crystal, who'd stretched out on the table and nearly fallen asleep, he said, "Are you ready, big girl?"

Crystal's sleepy eyes brightened. "Yes, Daddy."

She held her arms wide, and he scooped her into his. "Thank you, again, Dr. Chesapeake, for taking such good care of my little frog."

Crystal, barely awake, said, "*Ribbit*."

That had to be something special between them. Yep, Rayah would adore this little girl. And her father, Marisol thought mischievously. "You are very welcome. And call me Marisol, please. Dr. Chesapeake feels too formal around here."

After saying their goodbyes, Marisol contemplated on how she would make the introduction between Rayah and Roman. Even their names sounded great together. Maybe she could enlist the help of Kincaid. And speaking of Kincaid... She checked her watch. He hadn't called her all day. What was up with that?

"Marisol?"

She rotated and jolted from the greeting she received from a floral arrangement the size of a large bush. All of her favorite flowers decorated the enormous grouping: red roses, pink lilies, white hydrangeas, and a slew of other stems she couldn't readily identify. Ivy and curly twigs acted as fillers and all arranged in a beautiful crystal vase. The display looked as if it should occupy the center of a table at a *Preston Bailey* event. And looked as if it could have cost just as much as one of his arrangements.

"What is this?" Marisol asked Joni, the nurse holding the arrangement that was almost as big as the petite woman.

"It's for you," she said in a strained tone. "Could you please take it? It weighs as much as I do."

Marisol collected the exquisite bouquet and heaved it onto a nearby table. Retrieving the card, she tore into it.

Tomorrow, I'll love you even more, because every day you make loving you so easy. K-

Marisol's cheeks warmed at the beautiful words, then continued to read.

Meet me here at 7:00 p.m.

Following the words were two numbers: one labeled longitude, the other latitude. Was this a scavenger's hunt?

"How in the heck am I supposed to figure out where *here* is?" Marisol said.

Joni, who'd been peering over her shoulder, said, "Just plug the coordinates into your GPS. It'll take you right there."

Glancing at the clock, Marisol noted the time. *5:00 p.m*. That left her two hours to get home, shower, dress, and get to her destination. She wasn't sure where the coordinates would lead her, but the fact that Kincaid would be waiting at the end of her journey made the trip toward the unknown worth it.

Chapter 14

Kincaid surveyed the area he'd purposely chosen, losing himself in the pleasant memories he and Marisol had created there so long ago. Firefly Landing. The place they'd made love for the very first time. It surprised him that the wooded field hadn't been snatched up by developers and transformed into a new home community.

Closing his eyes, he recalled how Marisol's warm body felt under his. Inhaling deeply, he swore he could still smell the sweet tropical fruit fragrance she'd worn that night. He could definitely remember how his body had caved only minutes after entering her. Not an impressive first showing. But he'd gotten better.

Feeling the tightness in his boxers, he groaned. "*Slow, slow, slow.*" He had to continuously remind himself, especially when making love to Marisol was all he thought about anytime they touched. But he'd chosen to take a gentlemanly approach by courting and wooing her first.

Not a dark cloud lingered in the blue sky, and at a comfortable eighty degrees, the weather couldn't have been more perfect. Jumping back to the task at hand, he put the finishing touches on his set up. The layout looked just as he'd envisioned in his head. Taking a step back, he admired his work. By no means would anyone label him the most romantic guys in Indigo Falls, but with a little guidance from Pinterest, he'd done all right. Besides, it was the thought that counted, right?

Checking his watch, Marisol still had fifteen minutes.

He hoped he hadn't made it too difficult for her to find. Telling her where to meet him would have been much easier, but giving her coordinates provided an element of surprise. Of course, the closer Marisol got he knew she would figure out exactly where he was leading her.

The sound of crushing gravel drew his attention. Looking up to see Marisol driving into the open field caused a smile to curl his lips. Even from there, he could see the huge grin on her face through the windshield.

On approach, he opened the door and helped her out of the vehicle. "Wow. You look amazing."

"I wasn't sure how to dress." She chuckled. "I'm thinking I may have overdone it."

The fitted white dress tattered with dark blue flowers rode her curves like a race car rode a track. Overdone it, maybe. But he was not complaining. "It's perfect."

"Firefly Landing," she said. "What are you up to?"

Instead of answering her, he pulled her into his arms. Her pink painted lips too much to resist, he covered her mouth with his and kissed her long and hard. When she moaned, he vowed to hear much more of the sound. But not tonight. Tonight was all about romancing her. Laced with regret, he pulled away from Marisol's mouth before she had a chance to feel the swell in his pants. But when Marisol smirked at him, he knew it was too late.

"Is that a very firm cucumber in your pocket, or are you just happy to see me?"

He tossed his head back in laughter. "Very happy to see you," he said. "Very, very happy to see you." Capturing her hand, he led her to a black wrought-iron table with two matching chairs. Two plates, champagne glasses and utensils were arranged on top. Three mason jars sat in the center, filled with clear marbles, water, and a floating candle in each. Wheat-colored raffia bows were tied around the rims. The candles weren't necessary because plenty of light still remained, but it added to the ambience of the romantic scene in the middle of the grassy meadow.

"I hope you're hungry," he said, uncovering a delicious arrangement of fresh cut fruit, cheeses, veggies, and dips— a sweet whip for the fruit and a dill blend for the veggies.

"Wow. This is some spread," Marisol said, stealing a strawberry from the tray and lifting it to her mouth.

Kincaid swallowed the saliva that had formed from watching her beautiful lips close around the plump fruit. She had no idea what she was doing to him with a move like that. Or did she? Taming the beast, he said, "I had a little help from your aunt."

A look of surprise spread across her face. "Vaden knew about this?"

"Yeah, she did."

"And she didn't say one single word about it."

"Your aunt is good at keeping secrets."

A serious expression spread across Marisol's face. "Yes, she is."

Kincaid wanted to know what the sadness he saw in her eyes was all about, and eventually knew he would, but this moment was all about making her smile.

"My lady," he said in accented tongue, directing her into one of the chairs.

"Fancy," she said with an appreciative smile.

"Something smells great."

Kincaid grinned. "Dinner. It'll be ready soon."

Her brow furrowed. "Dinner? Are you cooking something?"

"Yes."

"But we're in the middle of nowhere and I don't see a grill."

"I can work magic." He winked.

Her eyes trailed to his lips. "Yes, you can." Meeting his gaze, she said, "What are we having?"

"Let me surprise you."

"You've already succeeded at doing that. Thank you for the flowers, by the way. I loved them."

Marisol crossed one sexy leg over the other, flashing her beautiful thigh. He fought the urge to drag his fingers over the exposed flesh, but couldn't curtail the image of peppering kisses along the inside of her thigh right before dipping his tongue deep inside her dripping—

"I guess this means you've gotten a little better at cooking, huh?"

"—wet." He chuckled. "I'm sorry. *What*...were you saying?"

Marisol tilted her head and eyed him awkwardly. "I said, I guess you've gotten better at cooking."

"What are you talking about? I've always been an excellent cook."

She arched an accusing brow.

"Okay. So I wasn't that good of a cook back then, but that has changed."

"We'll see," was all she said.

They spent the next twenty minutes on small talk. Getting to know new things about one another. Some of the things he'd learned about Marisol came as no surprise. Like her learning to play the guitar and violin. She'd always loved music. But the fact that she'd actually recorded and cut a CD did.

"You have got to let me hear it," he said.

"Not on your life. The studio guy and myself are the only two people who've heard it. And I plan to keep it that way."

"Why record a CD if you didn't want anyone to hear it?"

Marisol's eyes slid away from him and trained on her hands. "It was an outlet." Meeting his gaze again, she said, "It was therapeutic."

He nodded understandingly. Tonight, he wouldn't pry, but he couldn't guarantee the same for tomorrow. He wanted to know everything about Marisol he'd missed over the past ten years. That included the good, the bad, and everything in between.

"What about card making? Are you still doing it?" he asked.

"I haven't in years," she said with a hint of grief in her tone.

That was a shame, because she was so good at it.

An alarm chimed and drew their attentions toward his truck.

"You're about to be amazed," he said, pushing from the chair. "I'll be right back. Don't go anywhere." Kincaid started away, but stopped, backtracked, bent at the waist and pecked her gently. He made a sound like a thirst had been quenched, then headed away again.

Lifting the bed cover of his truck, then lowering the tailgate, Kincaid revealed two *NuWave* ovens he'd placed there to prepare the meal of ribeye steaks, lobster tails, asparagus, mushrooms, and potatoes.

Marisol laughed out loud. "I've seen those on an infomercial and came very close to ordering one." She laughed again. "I can't believe... You always know how to amaze me. This is the best date ever."

With everything perfectly arranged on a silver platter, Kincaid rejoined her at the table. "It's not a Chef G. Garvin creation, but—"

"But it's perfect," Marisol said. "So perfect." With tender eyes, she said, "Thank you."

After their meal, Kincaid instructed Marisol to relax as he cleared the table. When he rejoined her, she eyed him in that delicate way that always made him smile. "What?"

"This is the perfect date. I don't remember you being so creative."

"We didn't have Pinterest in those days."

"Wait, *you* have a Pinterest account?"

"OMG, doesn't everyone?" he said animatedly.

Marisol hollered in laughter. "I'm sorry. I'm sorry. I just can't believe Mr. Manly Man does Pinterest."

Kincaid ran a hand down the thin blue and white striped shirt he wore. "I am a man of many layers."

"I think I'm going to enjoy peeling you," she said with a smirk.

He was looking forward to doing a little peeling of his

own. Mainly clothes off. "Do you remember this place?" he asked before his imagination got him in trouble.

"Of course I do."

"What do you remember about it?"

Taking in her surroundings, Marisol said, "I remember that old beat up pickup truck that sat pretty much where your truck is parked now. I remember hundreds of fireflies swarming in the field around us. I remember you telling me how much you loved me right before we made love for the very first time." Her gaze settled on Kincaid. Staring into his eyes, she said, "I remember this place very well. How could I ever forget it? This is where I became a woman."

"Making love to you that night was beyond anything I could ever put into words."

Unbeknownst to Marisol, he'd been just as nervous as she had been. He'd never taken a girl's virginity.

"You were so gentle with me. I remember never wanting you to stop. I felt so connected with you. When I cried, you thought you'd hurt me." She closed her eyes. "God, that night was so beautiful. The mood, the fireflies glowing everywhere."

"Speaking of fireflies..." he said, because if he spoke of anything else, he would have had Marisol stretched out on the ground, reliving that night. He stood and held out his hand for her to take. Leading the way to his truck, he removed two mason jars, passing one to her.

The sky had started to darken, and before long, it would be pitch dark. Before they ended their night together, he wanted to do one last thing.

Marisol eyed the jar, then Kincaid. "You want to catch

fireflies?"

"Yes. Unless, of course, you're now too dignified to partake of such a thing." He smirked at the no-you-didn't-go-there look she tossed him.

"Let's do this," she said. "Good thing I chose to wear flats tonight, but too bad for you. You're going down."

"You've always been a trash talker," he said, wrapping his arm around her waist and pulling her close to him. Instead of kissing her, which was his first instinct, he allowed his eyes to take in every inch of her face. He admired everything he saw: the fine lines creasing her forehead, the tiny ones crawling from the corner of her eyes, the barely visible scar on the bridge of her nose, those delicious lips. Everything about her aroused him.

"Same wager?" he asked, catching her probing brown eyes on his lips again.

"Same wager," she confirmed, making him the happiest man alive.

Chapter 15

Marisol felt like a teenager as she and Rayah lay across her bed, chatting like schoolgirls. They were supposed to be packing what few things Marisol had accumulated for the move into her new house in two days, but they'd made the mistake of taking a "quick" break. That'd been an hour ago.

"Wait, wait, wait just one minute." Rayah came up on her elbow. "Are you serious? You and Kincaid were at the exact location where the two of you made love for the very first time, and you didn't get busy?"

Marisol jolted forward. "Keep your voice down," she warned. "Vaden's right next door in her sewing room. And no, we didn't get busy," she said in a hushed tone. Falling back on the bed with a sigh, she eyed the ceiling. Believe me, I wanted to. But Kincaid never made a move."

"You should have taken charge. Don't tell me you've become sexually repressed. That is not the Marisol Chesapeake I know."

No, it wasn't. Her relationship with her ex had changed her in more ways than one. He craved control in all aspects of their relationship, including the bedroom. They'd had sex when, where, and how he wanted. When she initiated any kind of foreplay, her advances were met with rejection. In the back of her mind, she'd been afraid Kincaid would do the same. Though, in her heart, she knew better. And then there was the taking it slow thing, which grew less and less appealing every day.

"Okay, so what did the two of you do, since you didn't

get busy?" Rayah said, returning to a reclined position.

A smile touched Marisol's lips. "We laughed a lot. Talked a lot. Caught fireflies—"

"Caught fireflies?"

"It's something we used to do." She thought about the many times they'd run the fields of Firefly Landing chasing the insects. It'd been endless fun. That hadn't changed.

"And what exactly did you do with them?"

"We counted them. Whoever had the most, won."

"Won what?"

Marisol drifted to the wager they'd made years ago and had renewed at Firefly Landing. "Forever," she said, butterflies fluttering in her stomach at the thought.

Rayah came up on her elbow again, a delicate expression on her face. "Forever?" she said in a tender tone.

Marisol nodded with tear-filled eyes. "Forever."

"Don't you dare cry, Marisol Chesapeake." Rayah's voice cracked. "Because if you start crying, I'll start. And it took me too damn long to do this face."

"Okay," Marisol said, batting her eyes.

The two women rested in silence for a moment or two, both lost in their own thoughts. Marisol had no idea what Rayah was thinking, but her thoughts were on Kincaid. Lately, she hadn't been able to think about much else.

"You know what I love, Rayah?"

"Other than Kincaid?"

She jostled her friend. "Yes, other than Kincaid. I love when I glance up from whatever I'm doing and Kincaid's staring at me. Our eyes hold one another's. Long, hard. I'm wondering what's going through his mind, and I'm sure he's wondering what's racing through mine. We don't speak. Not a single word. We just stare. Unwavering. In those moments, looking far beyond what my eyes can see, I can feel how much he truly loves me. It feels amazing. I'm so happy. I'm even card making again." Something she hadn't done in years, but since returning to Indigo Falls, she'd gotten a burst of creativity.

"I want that kind of connection with someone."

Now would have been the perfect time to interject Roman Meyers into the conversation, but something washed over Marisol. Something that brought on a bout of sadness. "Kincaid makes me feel like a new woman. I love that man with every ounce of who I am, but at the same time, I'm afraid to fully expose myself to him. I don't want to be hurt again, you know? Am I being ridiculous?"

"Yes," she said unapologetically. "Kincaid loves you. Anyone with at least one good eye can see that."

"I know he does. And that scares me, too. I'm trying so hard not to bring any baggage from my last relationship into this one, but it's hard not to wonder if it'll go bad like it did with Patrick." Marisol closed her eyes. "Patrick damaged me, Rayah."

"You're not damaged, Marisol."

"Yes, I am. For so long I allowed Patrick to make me feel like I was worthless. I stayed with him because I began to believe him. I felt like no one else would want me."

"But you know now that that's not true. And I'll be damned if I allow you to convince yourself that you don't deserve Kincaid's love. That you don't deserve this happiness. Fuck Dr. Patrick Sinclair with his psychotic ass. You should have let me put a hit out on him."

Marisol couldn't help but laugh at her friend's words. "You are too much."

"I'm serious. It's a good thing you didn't tell me about any of the hell you were going through. It would have ruined our friendship."

"Ruined out friendship? How?"

"Because I would have loaded up my vehicle with six of the burliest ex-cons I could find; I'm talking submarine size brothers. Driven them to Charlotte and watched them play a few rounds of tag on Patrick's ass."

Both women laughed.

Rayah draped her arm around Marisol's shoulders. "I love you, girl. More importantly, Kincaid loves you. Let him help you reverse the *damage* that's been done. Open up to him. Tell him everything you've gone through, and let his love heal you."

Rayah sounded a lot like Vaden with her advice. Before Marisol could respond, her cell phone chimed. Lifting it from the nightstand, she smiled at the screen. Kincaid had been out of town for the past week, and she missed him like crazy.

"Only one person can draw a smile like that. It must be your boo-thang," Rayah teased.

"Shut up," Marisol said with a wide grin.

Hey, beautiful. Had you on my mind. Like always. LOL. I know you're busy packing, but I just wanted to say hello and that I love you to the moon. I felt like you needed to hear that. K-

Yes, she did. Marisol typed her reply. *You've always had the perfect timing. I love you to the stars.* She filled three lines with hearts and puckering lips.

When her phone chimed again, Rayah said, "Are you two sexting?"

"No, we're not sexting." Marisol read his response. *I caught every one of those kisses you just tossed me. Btw, I think you have something on the porch. Talk soon.*

"On the porch?" Marisol mumbled.

Rayah glanced at the screen. "What's on the porch?"

Marisol shrugged. "I don't know. Come on."

Making haste down the stairs, Marisol tore through the screen door, closely followed by Rayah. When she came to an abrupt stop, Rayah collided into her, pushing her closer to the oversized cardboard box sitting there.

It would have looked like any ordinary cardboard box had it not had a gigantic red heart attached to the side facing them. The box was large enough to easily accommodate a large bean bag chair. A bean bag chair identical to the one she'd hinted to wanting as a housewarming gift.

"What are you waiting for, Marisol? Open it already," Rayah said, standing beside her.

"Okay, okay." Marisol flipped back the flaps and yelped, shuffling a step or two back. Resting her hand on her collarbone, she laughed at herself. Kincaid was full of surprises.

Bunches of balloons—yellow, blue, green, white, and two different shades of pink—floated from the box. He constantly amazed her. Thoughtful and creative. It was a

140

stimulating combination in a man.

A lone metallic silver note dangled from one of the hot pink balloons. Marisol neared the suspended bouquet and read the message aloud. "Your love keeps lifting me higher and higher. I can't wait until our date this weekend."

Rayah placed her hand over her heart and cooed.

Maybe Rayah was right. Letting Kincaid heal her with his love didn't seem like such a bad idea. She could already feel the wounds fading.

***

Kincaid chuckled at the reply text Marisol sent him. A screen filled with hearts and lips he guessed represented kisses. That woman had a way of making his day. Two stories up was not the time to be thinking about Marisol's sweet kisses. An erection pushing against his zipper might send the wrong message to his guys.

As hard as he fought it, his mind couldn't ignore how much he wanted her. On their date at Firefly Landing he'd wanted to make love to her so bad that he'd gotten a headache. And when she'd volunteered to massage his temples, the feel of her warm fingertips kneading him almost did him in.

Her body language suggested she'd wanted him too, but instead of acting on impulse, he'd resisted the desire to rip off all of her clothes, snatch her into his arms, kiss her like an untamed animal, then drive himself so deep inside of her that he would need a compass to find his way out.

"Boss. Hey, boss," Hector, one of his crewmen, called

from across the roof.

"Shit," he mumbled, looking down at the bulge at his crotch. "Yeah, Hector?" Kincaid called back, pushing down his hard-on.

"Could you please tell this fool that two roof vents won't be enough. We need at least four."

"*Fool*? Who the hell are you calling a fool? I have more sense in my left ball than you got in that globe-sized head of yours," Benicio, his other crewman, said.

Hector and Benicio fought like cats and dogs every day, all day. If it wasn't known, no one would ever believe they were brothers. Kincaid had spent damn near most of the day keeping them in their separate corners.

"We're doing five vent covers," Kincaid said, settling the dispute.

"Told you" Hector said.

"You said four, idiot," said Benicio.

Kincaid shook his head at the two men. They were going to drive him to drink on the job. "I'm about to toss you both from this roof if you keep it up," he said. "Could you manage not to kill each other for the next four hours?"

Though Tinsdale Roofing was adequately staffed, Kincaid loved getting his hands dirty on occasion. Nowadays, most of his time was usually spent visiting jobsites to make sure everything was running smoothly and none of his guys were goofing off. But today, he was actually filling in for one of his guys who'd needed time off. He'd be damned glad when the man returned. One could only take Hector and Benicio in small doses.

"It's all love, boss. It's all love."

The two men embraced as if they hadn't just spent the last three hours at each other's throats. Damn, he was glad he and Mason got along so well. Maybe he'd call him when he got back to the hotel to thank him for being such a good brother.

"Whatcha got planned for the weekend, boss?" Hector asked, wringing his sweat-drenched bandana.

"Yeah, boss, whatcha got planned for the weekend?" Benicio echoed.

"Didn't I just ask that?" Hector said, then rambled off something in Spanish and ended it with *loco*.

Kincaid disrupted Benicio's response by saying, "I have a date with my lady."

Hector and Benicio made kissing sounds with their mouths. Kincaid laughed at the two overly-animated clowns. When they started speaking in Spanish, gyrating their hips and moaning, Kincaid had a good idea of what they were saying. When he promptly informed them of how easily they could be replaced, both men sobered instantly.

Truth be told, Hector and Benicio were irreplaceable. They were two of the best workers he could ask for. Never complaining about arriving early or griping about leaving late, they were good examples for the rest of his guys. Soon—especially if business continued to grow at such a rapid pace—they'd both be running their own crews.

Straddling the ridge of the roof, Kincaid thought about the gift he'd had one of his boys deliver to Marisol's porch. It'd been hell trying to get all of those balloons to stay inside long enough for him to secure the flaps into place.

Thanks to Nona, he'd become addicted to Pinterest.

He thought about the meme he'd seen of a dark silhouette behind a frosted glass, warning to *save yourself* from the addictive website. He should have taken heed.

The balloons fitted the theme of their upcoming date perfectly. He wondered how she liked the gift. No sooner had the words traveled through his mind, his phone sounded with the tone he'd assigned to Marisol.

You keep this up, and I might just have to keep you around.

He keyed back, *Don't you remember? I'm yours forever.*

Chapter 16

Marisol had to admit, she loved the dates Kincaid planned for them. They were simple, but thoughtful. Nothing like the complex and all-for-show dates she'd suffered through for the past year. Kincaid made sure they always did things they both loved to do, as well as introducing her to things she didn't know she loved until they'd done them.

Fly-fishing. Who'd have thought she'd enjoy that so much. But she had.

After having lunch at Foley's Pizzeria, they'd ventured to Sugar Faye's Candy Shop. Where they were headed now, she had no idea. Kincaid prided himself on keeping her in suspense. Truth be told, she would've been happy simply spending the day indoors with him, snuggled in his arms after a long bout of lovemaking.

But he'd been adamant about taking her out, especially since they hadn't seen each other in over a week. Whatever he had planned, she hoped it ended in hot, passionate sex. And if Kincaid didn't make the first move, she would. *Enough waiting*.

They turned onto a rutted path curtained with trees on either side. A short distance later the dense bush opened up into a large field. The location reminded her of Firefly Landing, minus the display in front of them.

"Surprise," Kincaid said.

Marisol's mouth fell open, then she squealed. "A hot air balloon. I've always wanted to do this, Kincaid." With her eyes pinned to the massive structure anchored in the middle of the field, she said, "You are totally the best boyfriend ever." She laughed, realizing she sounded like a girl half her age, not the professional she was. Kincaid had a way of suppressing her serious side and bringing out the fun side in her.

Joining the individuals around the balloon aircraft, a tall, solid, white man with sun-kissed skin, a full head of white shoulder-length hair, and welcoming smile, introduced himself as Dan Wilson—the pilot of the aerostat, which she soon learned was the term for a lighter-than-air craft.

After meeting the crew chief, they were introduced to the members of the chase crew—the woman and two men tasked with tracking the balloon during flight and retrieving them once they'd landed.

"Have either of you been up before?" Dan asked.

They both shook their heads.

"But I'm super excited," Marisol added with a huge grin.

Releasing a jolly laugh, Dan said, "I like your spirit."

"Showoff," Kincaid said, jostling her playfully.

Dan took a moment to point out the three parts of the balloon. The envelope, burners, and basket. "The envelope is the actual 'balloon' portion. It holds the air that's warmed by the burners, which allow the craft to *float*, not fly. Hot air balloons *do not* fly," Dan said as if he was exhausted by the number of times he'd had to make the clarification.

After examining the cables that joined the envelope and the wicker basket, they climbed inside.

"Wow. There's a lot of instruments here," Marisol said.

Dan labeled them. "The Altimeter tells us how far above ground we are. The Variometer measures the vertical speed and tells us if we're moving up or down."

"Wouldn't we be able to see or at least feel which direction we're going?" Kincaid said.

Dan released another robust laugh. "At over a thousand feet off the ground, it's hard to judge anything at that altitude."

Kincaid nodded slowly as if it made more sense now. Dan pointed out a few more things, gave them a briefing that included the do's and don'ts, then they were off.

As they ascended, the view amazed Marisol. But the higher they floated, the shallower her breathing became. A flashback from a night she would never forget popped into her head, and she nonchalantly backed away from the basket's edge and closed her eyes in hopes of subduing the onset of queasiness.

You can do this, Marisol. You can enjoy this wonderful experience Kincaid has planned, dammit. Get yourself together.

Dan touched her arm, startling her to the point that she flinched. When her eyes popped open, both he and Kincaid were eyeing her with concern.

Dan squinted at her. "I've seen a lot of expressions, but the one on your face looks like pure terror. You okay? Didn't much think to ask if you were afraid of heights."

Kincaid cradled her face between his hands. "What's wrong?"

"I'm...just a little lightheaded, that's all. I'll be fine." Marisol forced a smile, then planted her face in Kincaid's chest. "I'm sorry," she said, her voice cracking with emotion. "You went through so much trouble. I don't want to ruin this experience for you."

"You're not ruining anything. Baby, you're shaking like a leaf," Kincaid said, draping his arms around her.

Nestled against his warm, solid chest, she fought the tears threatening to fall. "I'm so sorry," she said again, clinching tightly to the fabric of his shirt.

"Can we land?" Kincaid said to Dan.

Dan radioed to the chase crew. A short time later, they were back on solid ground. Loading into the awaiting black Chevy Tahoe, they were whisked away like celebrities.

The trip back to Kincaid's truck was made in silence. Kincaid held her hand, caressing the top with slow, delicate strokes with his thumb. Marisol's focus remained settled out of the window. Through the reflection in the glass, she witnessed each time he rotated to look at her. Clearly, he wanted to say something, but apparently, didn't know what.

Kincaid had to think she was crazy. In the past, heights had never been an issue. They'd ridden the highest roller coasters, zip-lined hundreds of feet in the air, jumped off steep cliffs into the water. All of that had to be running through his mind.

"We're here," Kincaid said softly.

After thanking the crew for everything, they headed to Kincaid's truck.

"I'm sorry, Kincaid."

"Come here," he said, pulling her into his arms. "Stop apologizing."

The feel of his warm arms soothed her frazzled nerves. "This was supposed to be a special day, and I ruined it," she said into his chest.

"You didn't ruin anything." He kissed the top of her head and chuckled. "When did you become afraid of heights?" He held her at arm's length. "Better yet, why didn't you tell me?"

"I didn't know I was until we were up there and I had a—" Her eyes slid away, and she studied her feet.

Kincaid tilted her chin upward. "You had a what?"

Staring into his caring eyes, she wanted to tell him everything she'd endured at the hands of her ex. It was just too much, too soon. Her eyes slid away again.

"Do you not trust me?" Kincaid asked.

"Why would you ask me that? Of course I trust you."

"At times it seems you don't. Not a hundred percent. Especially when you withdraw from me and go into your own little world, like you're doing now. I've tried to ignore it, but after today… I can't any longer. What's going on?"

"It's not you, Kincaid. I swear it's not."

"I want to believe you, Marisol, but…" He shrugged. "Communication is what ended us the first time. I want us to get it right this time. Anything you want to know, I'm willing to tell you. I want, need the same. I love you to the depths of my soul. Let me into yours."

The words felt serious. His expression certainly was. As much as she wanted to run as far away as she could from this conversation—at least for now—she had to face it.

They couldn't move forward if she didn't.

Marisol swallowed hard, then said, "I had a flashback of my ex threatening to toss me out of a helicopter and into the ocean." She could still feel the wind whipping across her face as she fought him to close the helicopter door. "It was after a birthday party for one of our colleagues. He'd had too much to drink and, as usual, he got violent." Spoken aloud, her painful past lost a small fraction of its potency.

Kincaid went still for a minute, that turned into two, that turned into what felt like an eternity. His hands scrubbed over his head. He seemed confused, staggered by what he'd just heard. Who could blame him?

Finally snapping from his stupor, his brows furrowed. "Did he ever hit you, Marisol?"

"I... He slapped me once." The blow had felt like she'd been hit with an iron fist. She hadn't even shared this with Vaden. "But it never happened again." Though a few times she'd feared it would.

Kincaid snatched the passenger's side door open with so much force Marisol thought it would come off the hinges. A vein bulged on the side of his neck, but he seemed to be trying to contain his composure.

"Kincaid—"

"Get in the truck, Marisol. Please."

Marisol didn't budge. "No. Not until you talk to me. Communication, remember?"

Kincaid struck the side of his truck. "You want to communicate? Okay. I'm taking you home," he said in an elevated tone. "Then I'm driving to Charlotte, finding that asshole and make him wish he'd never met you. I guarantee you he'll never lay a hand on another woman as long as he lives. Which might not be too much damn longer." His tone softened. "Now get in the truck, please."

"So you want to fight for my honor. You want to resort to violence. That won't make you any better than him, Kincaid."

"You can say that to me? And with a straight face?" Kincaid neared her. "This man— Why am I calling this punk a man? This *lowlife* laid his hands on you, Marisol." He flashed his palms. "Okay. You don't want me to confront him, fine. I'll just tell your brothers and let them handle it." He fished his cell phone from his pocket as he stormed to the driver's side of the truck.

Marisol hurried behind him, positioning herself in front of him. "You can't tell my brothers. They would kill him."

"What the hell did you think *I* would do?" he said, his eyes darkened with anger. "I don't get it. Why are you trying to protect him? Are you still in love with that bastard?"

His words spewed like acid that burned to her core. "I never loved him. I never loved any other man because I couldn't stop loving you."

Her words seemed to douse a lot of the fire that had burned in his eyes. In his head, she was sure he was asking himself if she didn't love Patrick, why had she stayed. It was the question she'd asked herself a million times.

"Please, Kincaid," she said, resting her hand on his cheek. "That's a chapter in my past." She smiled genuinely. "I'm moving forward, and it's all because of you."

Kincaid kissed her palm, then cradled her face and

kissed her deeply. When he pulled away, he said, "Let's get out of here."

"Okay."

When they arrived back at her place, she'd expected Kincaid to follow her inside once she popped the lock and entered the house. He didn't. The look in his eyes—exhaustion—and expression on his face—despair—made her heart bleed, because she'd been the one who'd done this to him. She'd burdened him with her problems, with her baggage.

Marisol rested her hand on the doorjamb. "Are you coming inside?"

"Nah." He pointed over his shoulder. "I'm gonna head home. I just wanted to make sure you got to your door safely," he said with the hint of a smile.

Her first thought was to protest, but she didn't. She half understood his need to be alone, or at least away from her. He had a lot to process. Heck, she could use some time alone herself.

"Okay. Call me when you get home? I want to make sure you made it to your door safely, too."

They shared a laugh that lacked much of the energy usually present between them.

Kincaid stepped forward, giving her a peck on the cheek. On the cheek. She tried to conceal how much his lack of affection bothered her. They didn't do pecks on the cheek; they did curl your toes and spine tingling.

Marisol grabbed the hem of his polo shirt as Kincaid attempted to walk away. When he faced her, she said, "I love you."

"I know. I love you, too."

Allowing the fabric to fall from her hand, Marisol folded her arms across her chest and watched him stroll away. Things had changed between them. Sighing, she backed into the house and eased the door closed. *Hot bath.* That's exactly what she needed. Actually, what she really needed was Kincaid's strong arms wrapped snuggly around her. But... She sighed again.

Marisol stripped as the tub filled. The steam rising from the water soothed her even before she stepped inside. The phone rang before she could settle into the liquid pleasure.

The caller ID flashed her brother's cell phone number. Answering, she said, "No, Jacen, Kincaid and I aren't having sex. And if we were—"

"Of course you're not, because Kincaid can't be in two places at one time," Jacen barked into the phone.

A horrible feeling washed over her. "What are you talking about?"

"I just stopped him running a hundred miles an hour. The second I let him go, he tore away again. Tell him when he gets back from Charlotte he's going to have a hefty ticket waiting for him."

"*Charlotte?*" Her stomach churned, and the air vacated from her lungs. Snatching in a breath, she whispered, "*No, no, no.*" When a bout of dizziness overcame her, she stumbled from the bathroom and into her bedroom, collapsing down on the mattress. "I have to go, Jacen."

"What the hell is—?"

She ended the call and with shaky hands dialed

153

Kincaid's cell phone. "*Please, please, please,*" she mumbled to herself. "*Answer, please.*" As she feared, the call rolled into voicemail. Trying again yielded the same result. On the fifth unanswered call, she left a message.

"Kincaid, baby, please don't do this. Don't stoop to his level. The reason I fell in love with you, the reason I've always loved you, is because of your gentleness, your heart of gold. You've always said you'd do anything for me. If that's true, come back to me. I need you right now. Come back to me. Please, Kincaid."

***

Judging by the number of times Marisol had called him, Kincaid was certain she'd spoken to her brother. When Jacen had stopped him, it was all he could do not to catapult from his truck and tear into him for not protecting Marisol from a monster. But he'd given Marisol his word he wouldn't tell any of her brothers what she'd gone through.

Jacen wasn't the one he truly wanted to take his aggression out on. It was Dr. Patrick Sinclair, and in a couple of hours, he'd get the chance. *What kind of man hits a woman?* Kincaid shook his head in disgust.

Even though she'd claimed he'd only slapped her, a vision of the faceless man raining down blows on Marisol flashed in his head every time he blinked. His grip on the steering wheel grew so tight that his knuckles cracked. Swallowing the painful lump lodged in his throat, he added a bit more pressure to the gas pedal.

"I should have been there to protect you," he said in a

low tone. "I should have been there for you." He drove his fist into the roof of the truck.

His cell phone rang again, breaking into his thoughts. Marisol's name flashed across the screen. Resisting the urge to snatch the phone up and tell her how much he loved her and how what he was doing was all for her, he remained focused on the road ahead and the rage coursing through his veins.

JOY AVERY

Chapter 17

A thousand scenarios plagued Marisol's thoughts for the past hour, each more devastating than the last. If anything happened to Kincaid, she would never be able to forever herself. God, why had she let him leave? Why hadn't she just—

The doorbell rang and she jolted. Sprinting to the door, she snatched it open. "Kin— Jacen? What are you doing here?" She'd expected him before now. Especially with the way she'd ended their call so abruptly.

Jacen was dressed in his official attire—khaki colored long-sleeved shirt, crisp olive-colored pants and tie, and black boots so glossy they practically glowed. The only thing shiner was the silver badge attached to his shirt. Even without the baton, pepper spray, or Glock .40-caliber at his waist, his commanding presence would force any criminal to think twice before crossing him.

"Damn. Don't seem so happy to see me," he said sarcastically.

Marisol glanced past him as if expecting to see Kincaid trailing him up the walkway. "It's not that... Come in."

They embraced once he stepped inside.

Jacen didn't crack a smile when he said, "What's going on with Kincaid? And why does whatever it is have you so upset?"

Marisol wrung her hands together, her mind reeling for a plausible explanation. "We—"

"*Sheriff*. Hey, Sheriff!" The dispatcher's voice boomed

over the radio attached to Jacen's shoulder.

Jacen clicked his two-way radio. "What is it, Wallace?" he said in an exasperated tone.

"Sheriff, that you?"

"Yeah, it's me, Wallace," Jacen said in an annoyed tone.

"Got us a little situation over at Merle B's. Clancy's making some kinda fuss 'cause Ms. Merle won't let him bring Sarah Belle inside. Said she can't refuse them service. Claims he's gonna burn down the whole town. I think he's off his meds again. You better hurry, Sheriff. It could get ugly."

"*Jesus Christ*. I'm on the way," he said into the radio.

Saved by the bell, Marisol thought. More like the *Belle*.

"Old man Clancy is going to be the death of me. I gotta go, sis, but this conversation isn't over."

She knew it wasn't. Trailing Jacen to the door, she said, "Did Mr. Clancy remarry? Who's Sarah Belle?"

On the porch, Jacen replaced his hat. "Sarah Belle's his pigmy goat. The death of me," Jacen reemphasized.

Though she wasn't in a jovial mood, she couldn't resist laughing. Shutting the door, she massaged her tight shoulders and decided to try Kincaid again. Thoughts of the trouble he was racing toward knotted her stomach. Patrick was on a first name basis with the police chief and mayor of Charlotte. They would bury Kincaid. She rested a shaky hand on her stomach as if to calm the quaking.

A tap at the door drew her attention. *Dammit*. Placing the phone down, she said, "What did you forget, Jacen?"

Marisol froze when she opened the door to see

Kincaid there. When he lifted a plastic bag, she recognized the odd-sized container instantly. "Ice cream?"

This brought back a mess of memories from their past. When they argued, Kincaid would leave to *"Get his head right,"* he'd say. It never failed, when he returned he'd bring her a container of her favorite ice cream. His way of apologizing. They'd sit on the floor and enjoy it together.

The more things changed, the more they stayed the same.

In a tired tone, he said, "It took me forever to find butter pecan."

Marisol cradled his face between her hands and eyed him as if she hadn't seen him in years. Draping her arms around his neck, she said, "Thank you."

Kincaid held her snugly. "How do I—? What do I—?"

Marisol's eyes filled with tears. "Just love me, Kincaid. Just love me."

He pulled away and eyed her. "That, I can definitely do."

They stood staring into each other's eyes. God, she wanted him. Wanted him so badly she couldn't think straight. Wanted him now. And she refused to wait another minute. The look in his eyes told her the wait was finally over.

She offered a silent thank you to whatever sex god who'd answered her prayer, then kissed him in a way that left no room for misinterpretation as to where she wanted this to lead. Like she'd hoped, Kincaid met her desperate need, her untamed desire. The bag containing the ice cream slipped from his hand, making a *thunk* when it landed on the Brazilian hardwood.

Hoisting her into his arms, he moved further into the house, pinning her against a wall. A moan escaped when he ground his hardness against her throbbing sex. Was it possible to want something more than she wanted air? Yes. That was hell, yes.

Their kiss—primal and hard—caused her lips to grow tender. The delicious pain only made her want more. Her gluttonous desire didn't wane when Kincaid pulled away. "*No, no, no.* Don't stop," she said in a huffed breath, her hungry mouth chasing his.

"The things I want to do to you." He shook his head slowly. "I want to make love to you all night. I want to kiss you all day. I want to hold you so close that our hearts beat in harmony. I want to make you scream my name until you're hoarse, make you come harder than you ever imagined you could." He kissed the tip of her nose. "But before I do any of those things, I want to touch you. Touch you in a way the bastard before me never could."

His words electrified her entire body. The idea of his strong hands exploring her caused a warm sensation to course through her. "Touching is good." When she dipped forward to kiss him again, he placed an index finger over her lips, slid it away slowly, then pecked her gently. His sensual way had her so sexually charged that she was sure her panties were soaking wet.

"I want to touch you in a way that when a warm breeze kisses your cheek..." he brushed a bent finger along the side of her face, "...you think of me." He glided his thumb over her ear. "I want to touch you in a way that

159

when the wind blows, you hear my voice whispering 'I love you' in your ear."

Marisol's breathing grew clumsy. Kincaid's words were beautiful, poetic. They aroused her far more than she imagined words ever could. Her skin prickled from the sensation of his fingers crawling along her arm.

"I want to touch you at night." He kissed her forehead. "I want to touch you during the day." He kissed her brow. "I want to touch you seven days a week." He kissed her jaw line. "And when I touch you…" he positioned his mouth inches from hers, "…it's going to drive you absolutely insane."

He captured Marisol's mouth and kissed her like his life recharged with each stroke of his tongue against hers. The kiss was potent, deliberate; it was delicious, satisfying. Her entire body blossomed like one of Vaden's flowers.

When Kincaid pulled away, Marisol panted like she'd just run a marathon. His breath was just as unsteady as hers. She swallowed hard, recalling his very arousing claims. "W—" She cleared her throat. "Where are you planning to touch me that will achieve all of that?" she asked.

Kincaid's lips curled into a smile. He dragged a finger over her chin, down the column of her neck, and over her collarbone. Resting a flat hand over her breast, he said, "Your heart."

The words dumbfounded her, but the sternness of his gaze anchored her to reality. "*My…heart?*" she said, her thoughts swirling in a hundred different directions. How did she respond to something so…so…beautiful? How did she translate how deeply she'd been *touched* by his words?

She rested her warm, shaky hands on the sides of Kincaid's face. "That moment..." A tear escaped down her check. "That moment when you understand why no other relationship lasted. My long, crooked road was clearly designed to lead me back to you. I love you, Kincaid Tinsdale. I love you for being you. And I love you for loving me, renewing me."

Touching her lips to his, she kissed him delicately, then pulled away. "You've already touched my heart. Now, I want you to touch other things. I want to make love to you, Kincaid. I don't want to wait another second, minute, hour, or day." She gave him another gentle kiss. "Let's christen my new home. Make love to me."

A beat later, Kincaid stepped away from the wall. She'd never felt safer in a man's arms than she did now. The warmth radiating from his solid chest, the feel of his strong arms holding her close—claiming her as his—heightened her arousal.

Not taking their eyes off one another's, they moved in silence. Why use words when the intensity of their stares spoke volumes. Plus, no words were needed to express the hunger threatening to consume them both.

Instead of heading to the bedroom, Kincaid lowered to the floor. With his body blanketing her, she stared into his eyes and shivered at the level of yearning she witnessed in them. Yes, she wanted this man more than her next breath—absolutely and completely—but the moment became about something far more than sex.

Taking in every inch of his beautiful face: thick, dark brows, hypnotic eyes, juicy lips she craved to kiss. "I love you so much it scares me," she said, in little more than a whisper.

"Don't let loving me scare you. Let the knowledge of my loving you make you capable of facing your greatest fear. My love will always shield and protect you."

"I wish I could go back in time and erase the goodbye. I can't, but I'll spend every tomorrow making it up to you."

At her words, something far beyond want, well beyond need, flashed in Kincaid's eyes. It wasn't necessary for him to define what it was. The expression on his face—intense, powerful—revealed he felt the same way.

"Touch me," she said.

Kincaid started at her temple and kissed his way along the side of her face, speed clearly not a factor. His unhurried kisses moved along her jaw line and to her lips. He didn't ravish her mouth, not like she'd wanted him to do; instead, a tender peck was all she got. A peck that was so sensual that it was all she needed. At least for the moment.

When she tilted her head back, Kincaid kissed the base of her throat. His tongue traveled a path to her chin. The sensation surging through her body caused her to moan slow and deep.

"Look at me, Marisol," he said.

She wasn't sure at what point she'd closed her eyes, but she opened them and met his gaze.

"Do you believe us both returning to Indigo Falls was a coincidence?"

"I've asked myself that same question a dozen times. I don't know, Kincaid. What I do know is that prior to returning, I felt as if I'd been holding my breath. Being here, being with you...I finally feel like I'm breathing again."

"What *he* wasn't, I'll be. I'll be that and much more. Just tell me what you want and I'll give it to you."

In a delicate tone, Marisol said, "I want to be your ultimate desire."

Her request seemed to light a fire inside of him. Stripping away the oversized shirt she wore, Kincaid tossed it aside. The coolness against her skin felt great, because the rest of her body was on fire. He smiled down at her bare breasts. A beat later, his warm, wet lips closed over one of her throbbing nipples. A deep moan echoed through the house, then another. His this time.

After taking pleasure in both breasts, he trailed kisses down her torso, stopping at her panties. Hooking both thumbs inside, he slinked the material down her body. Blood whooshed in her ears, a result of her unbridled yearning. Instead of touching her like she craved, Kincaid stood.

"Where are you going?"

Silently, Kincaid stared down at her. His eyes raked over every inch of her bare form. Her physique was far from that of a swimsuit model's and wasn't as firm as it'd been years ago, but the admiration she witnessed in his eyes made that a-okay, made her feel flawless. The appreciative gaze empowered her.

"Damn," he said in a low, tender tone. "You are absolutely beautiful."

Kincaid's words dispelled every negative word her ex had ever muttered about her imperfect body. When Kincaid begin to undress, Marisol's breathing slowed to a crawl. Yes, she'd seen him shirtless plenty. Had followed the trail of fine, curly black hairs as far down as she could see countless times. But she had yet to see the part of him that truly made him a man. Lust held her in a stranglehold, its vice-like grip tightening the second his boxers fell to the floor.

"Yes." She laughed when she realized she'd said it out loud. And so did he.

More of him existed than she remembered. Her appreciative stare took in all of him. *Much more*. Sucking her bottom lip between her teeth, her eyes climbed the length of his body and settled on his dark, hungry eyes.

Returning to the floor, he positioned himself next to her. Close enough for his delicious lips to tickle the hairs on her ear, he whispered, "I want to learn your body inside and out."

He dragged his index finger down the center of her chest in a slow, provocative manner that made her nipples tighten to the point that both felt as if they would crack.

"If I'm doing something you like..." he paused, "say...yes."

Her blood pressure rose to an unsafe level and her breathing labored. "O...kay." A second later, he nipped her earlobe and it sent a jolt through her body. "*Yes*."

"I haven't started yet," he said with a chuckle. He kissed her behind the ear. "I love the way you knead at this pretty lobe when you're not being a hundred percent truthful."

So Vaden hadn't been the only one to pick up on her tick.

When Kincaid kissed a path to her mouth, chin, down the column of her neck, and across her collarbone, yes rang out like bullets from an automatic weapon. By the time he closed his lips over one of her hardened nipples again, she was too dizzy with need to do much more than secure her next breath. And even that was difficult.

"Do you not like that?" he asked, never halting from the delicious pleasure.

"Mmm hmm," she hummed, her body so ignited it felt as if she was going to lose consciousness. "I...like it all."

Kincaid continued to kiss all around her breast, but paused briefly. The crinkling of the plastic bag the ice cream had come in, forced her to crack one eyelid open just in time to see him pulling the bag toward them.

"What are you—?" Before she could finish the thought, Kincaid had her covered in melted ice cream. Fine bumps rose over her skin and she shivered. "I can't believe—" The feel of him lapping up the sticky cream halted her objection.

He licked, nipped, kissed her. His fingers glided down her body and found the moisture between her legs. "*Yes, yes, yes,*" she cried out as two long, stiff fingers glided in and out of her slowly while his thumb made delicate circles over her hardened sex bead.

"It feels like you want me," Kincaid said, his mouth now hovering over hers, his stern eyes tracing every inch of her face. "Do you?"

"*Yes,*" she said, in an anxious tone. "*Yes.*" When his lips smashed to hers, she eagerly allowed his tongue entry. His sweet taste, his determination, ushered her closer to the edge of sexual insanity. "Kincaid..." she moaned as he pulled away from her mouth. "I'm about to—" A whimper escaped as her body drew closer and closer to succumbing to the masterful maneuvering of his fingers.

Through the cloud of her impending orgasm, Marisol gave little thought to Kincaid's body inching down her. Reckless awareness set in the second his mouth resumed the duty of his thumb. Her hands glided over his head as she welcomed every deliberate stroke of his tongue.

She fought the sensation creeping up her spine, ignored the rapid thud of her heart against her ribcage, attempted to tune out the *whoosh* of blood in her ears, but Kincaid's warm mouth savoring her was too much to handle. And when he sucked her between his lips, her body exploded.

The orgasm slammed full speed into Marisol, causing her back to arch off the floor. Cries of ecstasy filled the entire house. Kincaid continued to work her with his mouth as he hummed, "Mmm hmm," over and over. With each tease of his tongue, the muscles between her legs contracted more. This couldn't be her body. Her body wasn't capable of feeling this level of rapture. At least it hadn't before now.

After what felt like an hour, the orgasm faded, leaving her spent. The rustle of foil alerted her to the fact that this pleasure had only just begun. Kincaid's body blanketed hers, most of his weight supported by his elbows.

"Although I didn't hear a yes," he said, staring down at her, "something tells me you enjoyed that."

"Could you not taste my yes," she countered, causing a

roguish smile to spread across his face. When he sucked his lips between his teeth and hummed, "Mmm," the muscles between her legs twitched.

"Kiss me," she said.

"I'm not sure I want to share any of this yummy flavor."

Marisol cradled his face between her hands. "I promise you, anytime you want a taste, you can have a taste," she said, pulling his head to her mouth. "Now, kiss me."

"How could any man resist an offer like that?"

As with every time their mouths connected, a tingle traveled from the top of Marisol's head to the bottom of her feet. But this time, the kiss meant so much more. This kiss was ushering them to the next level of their relationship. This kiss took her breath away. Or maybe it was the sensation of Kincaid's solid shaft gradually filling her.

"*Ahhh*." She dug her nails into his moist back.

His head nestled in the crook of her neck. Groaning a sound of pure satisfaction, he said, "I've missed you." Warm lips pressed against her skin, kissing her once, twice... "I'm home."

"I forgot making love could feel like this," she said.

Kincaid brought his gaze to hers. "This feeling is the only feeling I want you to remember," he said, guiding her legs further apart and driving himself even deeper inside of her.

Every stroke, every kiss, contributed to the heat pooling in her core. His motion—smooth, at first—grew faster, harder. She welcomed every thrust of his hips, every grind of his pelvis against her.

Kincaid rested his forehead against hers. "You fit me like a glove."

She kissed the tip of his nose. "Come with me."

"I'll follow you anywhere."

And he did, their cries of ecstasy rattling the walls.

Resting in Kincaid's arms, Marisol understood how it felt to fly. How could she have ever believed there could be any other man for her?

Chapter 18

At three in the afternoon, the only thing Marisol had accomplished for the day was showering. She hadn't even bothered getting dressed. Instead, she'd climbed back in bed with only a pair of red boy-short underwear and yanked her favorite fleece blanket up to her chin, despite it being close to ninety outside.

The faint scent of Kincaid's cologne lingered on the covers, reminding her of their night together. They'd made love until a ridiculous hour. Before he'd left that morning, he'd served her breakfast in bed—French toast with sourwood honey.

Remembering how he'd swirled his finger through the light amber-colored sweetness and painted her nipples, made her tingle. Recalling how he'd licked it off slowly caused the junction between her thighs to swell with arousal.

God, she missed him. Something about being in the house alone made her sad. Maybe it was the weather. Torrential rain had started a little over two hours ago and showed no signs of letting up anytime soon. Rain always made her gloomy.

She thought about texting Kincaid, but decided not to bother him while he was out with his boys, especially since he'd wanted to stay in bed with her, but she'd been the one to push him out the door. Actually, bother him *again* would be more accurate. When she recalled the text she'd sent an hour ago, his reply made her smile. A shot of one of the many selfies they'd taken lying in bed that morning.

Marisol's eyes drifted shut, but popped open when she thought she heard the front door creak open. Her ears perked and a wave of fear shrouded her. Before she had the opportunity to craft some outlandish scenario in her head, Kincaid appeared in the doorway.

Coming up on her elbow, she said, "Kincaid? What are you doing here?"

Without a word, Kincaid kicked out of his shoes, peeled off his socks, stripped down to his boxers and climbed in bed. Eye-to-eye with her, he said, "You sent me a text that said I miss you."

"I did miss you."

"You don't do *I miss you* texts. You do *I love you* texts, *I can't wait to see you* texts, *I'm thinking about you* texts, but never *I miss you* texts. And when you did, I knew you needed me. Plus, I know how rain depresses you."

He knew her so well. "You can't run to me every time it rains."

"Maybe not, but I'm here now," he said.

She didn't need a reminder of how much Kincaid loved her, but daily, he did something that did just that and reminded her that she was the luckiest woman on earth. "I always need you."

"Tell me what's wrong," he said, kissing her forehead.

How could she tell him when she didn't even know herself? When the rain started, so had her tears. "I don't know," she said, a lone tear escaping out the corner of her eye. She shrugged. "The weather?"

Kincaid swiped his thumb across her cheek. "You just

need me to hold you and whisper something sweet into your ear."

Yes, she did. "That could work." Repositioning so that they spooned, Marisol said, "I feel better already, but you did mention something about whispering something sweet in my ear."

He released a sexy chuckle, then kissed the crook of her neck. "I love you."

"Mmm. That's pretty sweet."

He kissed the space below her lobe. "I need you."

"That's pretty sweet, too."

He kissed the edge of her ear. "You're the best thing that's happened to me in a long time. You keep saving me, Marisol Chesapeake."

That gave her a sugar high. "Tell me a story, Kincaid. Something beautiful."

He snuggled her even closer. "I fell in love in a dark and dense forest."

She smiled, liking the introduction. "Really? Tell me more."

"I'd just lost my mother to cancer. I was hurting so bad and didn't know what to do with all of the emotions swirling inside of me."

His grip tightened around her, and she knew he was reliving some of that pain.

"I needed to get away, be alone. I hopped on my bike, peddled as hard as I could to the woods outside of town. Not knowing what else to do, I just screamed at the top of my lungs, releasing some of the pain I felt. I thought I was alone." He chuckled. "I wasn't."

Kincaid's mother's death had been the catalyst that'd brought them together. Marisol allowed her thoughts to drift back in time. She'd been riding her bicycle outside of town when she'd heard the most tortured scream she'd ever heard in her life.

Instead of peddling away as fast as she could, she gravitated toward the source. Weaving her way into the forest, she'd found a sullen Kincaid with his forearm propped against a tree, his forehead resting against it. When she'd called out to him, he faced her with red, swollen eyes and tear-stained cheeks. Her heart chose him then and there.

She'd been at the right place, at the right time.

"I heard the voice of an angel behind me. Soft, kind, soothing. '*Do you need a friend*?' she asked me. We talked for hours. We had so much in common it was ridiculous. She became my best friend. And though she played hard to get, my charms finally won her over, and she became my lover; she became my life. The end."

Marisol smiled, another tear rolling from her eye. This time it didn't represent sadness. "Sounds like a fairytale."

"Oh, it was. It *is*."

Rotating to face him, she said, "Does it have a happily ever after?"

Kincaid came up on his elbow and stared down at her. "You bet your ass it does."

***

Kincaid glanced over at Marisol in the passenger's seat

as they drove up the winding driveway leading to the place he would soon call home. She was more focused on the scene outside of the window, than the fact that he was admiring her. God, he loved this woman.

Refocusing his attention ahead, he was impressed with the progress that had been made. It had come a long way since the last time he'd been there. According to the builder, they would be done in another two months or so.

Parking behind an electrical truck, Kincaid moved to Marisol's door and opened it. When she stepped out, he couldn't resist stealing a sweet kiss from her.

Ending the hungry kiss, Marisol said, "Kissing me like that could get you in trouble."

With a wink, he said, "I've been known to be a troublemaker." When she dragged her thumb across his bottom lip to remove the pink lipstick she'd transferred, he sucked her finger into his mouth. "Damn, I can't wait until they're done with this house. I plan on making love to you in every room."

"I'm looking forward to it." Marisol looked past him and at the house. "You have your work cut out for you. This place is huge. Two or three families could live in that sucker."

"Or just one big one." He eyed her for a moment to see if she'd picked up on the hint. By the inquisitive look in her big, brown eyes, she had. "Come on."

Taking her by the hand, he led her toward the house, stopping directly in front of the massive two-story, all brick structure. Wrapping his arms around her from behind, he kissed the crook of her neck. "What do you think?"

"I love it. What goes there?" She pointed to a large circle bordered by decorative rocks.

"A fountain."

"That'll be beautiful."

"The house will have a state-of-the-art kitchen, a breathtaking master bath, a master walk-in closet that would give any woman an orgasm," he said, kissing the back of her head.

"Really? Well, that sounds like a place I'd like to visit."

"I was thinking something a little more permanent."

Marisol rotated in his arms. "Kincaid...?" She studied him a moment. "Are you trying to ask me to move in with you?"

"Yes, I am. We spend practically every night together already. It doesn't make sense to have two mortgages."

A soft smile touched her lips. "You want to share your space with me?"

"I want to share my life with you. This house is just the beginning."

Marisol eased out of his arms. Reading her body language—nervous, unsure—he knew he'd given her a lot to swallow. Possibly too much, by the choked expression on her face.

"I know it's a big step, but I—"

"Okay."

Kincaid cocked a brow. "O...kay, you'll move in with me or okay something else?"

Marisol laughed. "Okay, I'll move in with you."

As happy as he was by her answer, still, he didn't want her to do this only because she knew it would make him happy. "Are you sure? I'd understand if you said no. I don't want you to feel like I'm pressuring you or anything. I really want you to be—"

She placed her index finger over his lips. "Are you trying to rescind your offer, Mr. Tinsdale?"

"No. Hell, no."

"Good, because I think I'm going to like it here."

"Correction. You're going to *love* it here." He claimed her in his arms again. "This is the start of our happily ever after."

Chapter 19

Oh, no. Marisol's posture stiffened as her eyes scrolled over the text on the screen. If there was one thing you didn't want, it was to be featured in one of Ernestine's posts. It usually bordered embellished truth and outright fiction. How in the hell had she and Kincaid ended up in the woman's crosshairs? She huffed. "That woman and her blog."

"What?" Kincaid asked, finishing his bowl of cereal.

"Listen to this. The walls are talking, and they're saying love surely seems to be in bloom for Marisol Chesapeake and Kincaid Tinsdale, both of whom were recently spotted engaged in some serious lip action outside of Sugar Faye's Candy Shop."

When Kincaid sniggered, she shot him the evil eye. He lifted his hand in surrender. She continued. "This, of course, is in addition to the reports of a hot and steamy moment the two shared in the parking lot of Lady V's Diner. Will this lead to wed—?"

Marisol stopped again when Kincaid burst out laughing. Although Ms. Ernestine had recalled all of the details accurately—thus far—did she have to make it sound so scandalous?

"Imagine what she'd have written had she peeped through the bedroom window last night," Kincaid said with another burst of laughter.

"It's not funny, Kincaid Tinsdale." She smirked. "But if you want something to laugh about, here you go." She cleared her throat for effect. "We were all rooting for the reuniting of these two childhood sweethearts. But some feared Kincaid's stalker-like behavior would scare our sweet Marisol away. Luckily—"

"*Stalker-like behavior*? Let me see that." Kincaid took the iPad from Marisol and scanned the screen. He shook his head. "That woman shouldn't be allowed near anyone's keyboard."

Marisol leaned against the oversized island in Kincaid's kitchen. "This is all your fault, you know. All of your public displays of affections."

Kincaid placed the iPad down and snatched Marisol into his arms. "You enjoy every second of it." He pecked her gently. "Besides, I wanted to see what was sweeter: those jellybeans or your kisses."

He was right. She did enjoy it. It'd taken a little time for her to get comfortable with Kincaid pulling her into his arms and kissing her smack-dab in the middle of the town square, and she'd been a bit apprehensive. But when she realized he wasn't going to stop showing the world—or at least Indigo Falls—how much he loved her, she'd adjusted.

"And?" Marisol asked, wrapping her arms around his neck. "What was sweeter?"

"Hands down..." he kissed the tip of her nose, "...the jellybeans."

"The jellybeans, huh?" She playfully struggled to free herself from his embrace, then growled humorously when he wouldn't let her go. Which was okay with her, because she loved being in his arms.

"You know I'm only kidding." He kissed the tip of her

nose again. "There's nothing on this earth sweeter than your kisses."

"Aww." She pressed her lips to his gently, then pulled back. "Mmm, what's that?" She ran her hands slowly across the swell in the front of his pants.

A roguish grin crawled across his face. "I don't know. Whatever it is, it seems to happen every time I get too close to you. Maybe if I step back—"

Marisol grabbed a handful of his shirt. "No, you don't," she said, yanking him back to her.

"Oh, yeah. I like it when you get rough. It turns me on."

"You like it rough, huh?"

Well, so did she. And in a million years she never would have imagined admitting that. For so long, rough had meant something totally different. But she loved Kincaid's form of rough. His rough wasn't *rough*. Not the type of rough associated with pain. His rough was absolute pleasure...*rough*. The kind of rough that made her come as hard as a launching rocket.

Marisol smoothed her hands down the sides of his face. "No man has ever looked at me the way you look at me. The way you've always looked at me."

He kissed the back of her hand. "That's because no man has ever loved you the way that I love you. I can guarantee you that."

He rotated her until her butt was pinned against the island, then captured her mouth in a kiss that caused her entire body to heat. Tasting him, his tongue, his teeth, the sweetness of the cereal he'd eaten, made her want to taste more of him.

Breaking away from his mouth, she tugged at the hem of his shirt until it was over his head and lying on the floor like a puddle of chocolate milk. The feel of him under her fingertips—warm, solid—made her nipples bead inside of her bra. She pressed her lips against the stubble of his jaw and nibbled gently. A moan escaped from him when she nipped him gently on the neck.

"God, you smell amazing," she said, kissing his Adam's apple.

Kincaid's hands roamed all over her: her back, her ass, her hips, her breasts—his breasts—he constantly reminded her. Each swipe of his hand increased her longing to have him inside of her, but she didn't rush getting to that point.

Running her tongue in the dip of his collarbone, she continued to his pec. After she'd kissed the letters that spelled out her name, she found his nipple with her teeth and nibbled gently, making him shiver.

Kissing her way back up his body, Marisol pressed her lips to his again. While they shared a gratifying kiss, she stroked his hardness through the black gym shorts he wore. They moaned together when his shaft twitched in her hands. She loved when he made it do that.

Needing to feel actual flesh, she snaked her hand inside his boxers. He released a sound of pleasure when she held him in her hand and squeezed gently. She wasn't sure the jerk she felt this time was voluntary or not. Either way, it did something to her.

"I want to taste you," she said, lowering to her knees, pulling his shorts and boxers down with her.

Everything about Kincaid's body was beautiful, but his shaft—long, thick, and hard as tempered steel—was magnificent. As a tease, Marisol ran her tongue down his length, back up and over the tip. The move drove him crazy.

"Shit," he said in a low, throaty tone. "I want you so damn bad I'm not sure I can handle this."

They would soon find out.

When Marisol took him into her mouth, he wobbled as if he'd lost balance. Each time her lips glided over him, the sound he made became more primal. He threaded his fingers through her hair and moved his hands with the same rhythm of her slow glide up and down his length.

"This feels amazing," he said, "but I can't wait another second. I want you. Come here," he said, pulling her to her feet."

He undressed her with the speed of a cheetah securing its next meal. *Mmm*. She liked that analogy. If Kincaid was the cheetah, it meant *she* was the meal. And she loved the way he feasted. Although, with his eagerness, she doubted he would spend time on foreplay.

Marisol gasped. "What are—?" Before she could get the words out, Kincaid hoisted her onto the chilly marble island. "*Cold*," she said, in a yearning tone.

"We're about to heat it up," he said, guiding her back onto the solid slab.

"We eat off this counter, Kincaid."

"Precisely," he said with a wink, lowering his head to take one of her nipples between his lips.

"*Mmm*." She arched into his mouth. "I thought you wanted me so badly that you couldn't stand it."

"And I plan to have you," he said, never removing his lips from her.

With his free hand, Kincaid cupped the breast he wasn't gliding warm tongue strokes over and brushed his thumb over the nipple. It sent a wave of warm sensations coursing through her. His lips and hands caressed every inch of her as he made his way down to the valley between her legs.

When his stiff tongue twirled around her clit, she sucked in a sharp stream of air. It was all she could do to hold on and not topple over the edge, but every delicious stroke of his tongue brought her closer and closer.

The air in the room grew thick, her breathing shallow. Blood *whoosed, whoosed, whoosed* in her ears, and her toes curled tight enough to snap the bones. She didn't need to tell Kincaid where or how to tease her; somehow he always knew the exact spot that would send her catapulting off the cliff of ecstasy. She fought, but the orgasm claimed victory, elevating her to an all new level of rapture.

Nothing would escape. Not a scream; not a cry; not a whimper. Her body held her vocally hostage. The only things reassuring her she hadn't dropped into a coma was her trembling legs, and the sound of rustling foil. When had he gone for a condom?

The feel of Kincaid blanketing her body helped to guide her out of her stupor. He eased inside her slowly, releasing a guttural moan that vibrated through her body. Each stroke gained more speed, more energy. His thrust became *rough*, and she cried out, "*Yes*" with each plunge of passion.

Greed consumed her, and she demanded more of him. He complied, positioning both her legs over his shoulders and practically stood up inside of her. Deeper, swift strokes ushered her closer and closer to the edge. Literally. Because each powerful stroke shifted her on the island. The pleasure coursing through her overshadowed the fear of plummeting to the floor.

A beat later, her body spiraled out of control. The sensation of a thousand lightning bolts electrified her. Kincaid nearly toppled over the side when her back bowed off the hard surface.

Securing his grip, he said, "I'm right behind you, baby. *I'm...right...behind you.*"

After three of four more powerful strokes, he released a growl that had to escape from the depths of his soul.

***

Kincaid groaned his objection when Marisol attempted to escape his arms. Of all places, they'd fallen asleep on his kitchen island. Marisol's warm body snuggled against his kept his mind off the fact that the marble was cold as ice cubes. He'd welcomed the cold earlier, when Marisol had him sweating like a man on the chain gang in the dead of summer.

"Where are you going?" he asked in a groggy voice.

Marisol kissed his chin. "We have to meet Mason and Nona in an hour, remember?"

"Damn. I forgot about that," he said, scrubbing his hand over his head. Tugging at her arm playfully, he said,

"Can't we cancel? They'll understand." He'd much prefer they spend the remainder of the afternoon on their "deserted" island.

"No, we can't cancel. Nona really wants us there for the cake tasting. You know how emotional she's been lately. She'd probably burst out crying if we didn't show."

Marisol had a point. When they'd visited Nona and Mason the other night, Nona had cried for twenty minutes following one of those animal cruelty commercials. Were all pregnant women so emotional? Would Marisol cry at a commercial? Heck, what was he saying? She cried at commercials now and wasn't even pregnant...yet. He laughed.

"What's funny?"

He rested his elbows on his bent knees. "Nothing."

After a beat or two, she shrugged off his laughter. "Plus, you know I'm not missing an opportunity to eat some of Janelle's confectionary creations. That women works magic with a mixing bowl. Did she say when the cakery is opening?"

"Another three months of so. My guys start work on the roof next month."

"Her lemon supreme cupcakes filled with lemon curd are to die for. I could eat a thousand of those things. *Mmm.*"

"Keep moaning like that and I just might get jealous."

She leaned forward for a kiss. He was more than willing to oblige. When she pulled away, a sound of satisfaction escaped her pouty lips. He loved the sound now just as much as he had hours earlier when he'd been so deep inside of her that he damn near lost his mind.

"Don't worry, baby. That cupcake *ain't got nothing on you*."

Marisol strolled away and he watched her move down the hall. Her ass jiggled, filling him with a lustful heat. Was it normal for him to constantly want to make love to her?

"Hey," Marisol said.

Drawing his eyes away from her butt and up her torso, his eyes lingered a second or two on her plump breasts. They called to him to be licked, suckled, caressed. He finally settled on her face, laughing at the narrow-eyed gaze she tossed at him. Raising his hands in mock surrender, he said, "Hey, you can't fault a brother for admiring what's his, can you?"

A smile crept across her face. If he didn't know any better, he'd have thought she liked being claimed by him.

"Care to join me?"

He bit into his lower lip. As much as he wanted to catapult toward her, he knew if he followed her into that bathroom, they definitely would not make it to Janelle's for the cake tasting. At least, not on time.

Kincaid swung his long legs over the edge of the island. "You and I both know if I follow you in, we're not coming out anytime soon. You're insatiable, woman."

"Only you know how to feed my hunger. But…" she pouted, "…you have a point." She started away again, but stopped. "Oh, I'm expecting a call from Kisses and Cuddles concerning a custom order I placed for baby Abigail. I don't want to miss the call. Do you mind being my answering service? I'll reward you later," she said with a brow bounce.

"Woman, you better lock yourself inside the bathroom. You're seriously making me reconsider my previous decision."

Marisol posed in a sexy stance, then darted away when he came off the counter. "That woman," he said, shaking his head.

Smoothing his hand over the marble, he smiled at the things that'd taken place on the slab. Maybe he'd have the entire structure dismantled and moved to their new place. *Their new place*. That made him smile again, only this time much wider. What in the hell had he done to deserve this much happiness, this second chance with Marisol? Whatever it was, fortune favored him.

Scrubbing his hand over his face, he captured a delicious scent of Marisol's essence. To hell with it. Mason and Nona would understand their tardiness. Heck, people had "car trouble" all of the time. He took off down the hall, but before he could reach the bathroom, Marisol's cell phone rang.

"Damn. Talk about horrible timing." He'd almost allowed it to roll into voicemail, but remembered the call Marisol was expecting for Cuddles, Cuddle Kissers. *Something like that*.

Snatching up the cell phone, he said, "Hello?"

"Hello?" The masculine voice greeted him in accented English. "Is Marisol Chesapeake available, please?"

This caller sounded too dry for a baby store operator. Kincaid glanced at the caller ID. Area code 916. Where in the hell was that? "I'm...sorry, she's not. May I take a message?"

"Yes. Please have her contact Doctor Ralph Orenstein at the Sacramento County Coroner's office. I'm eager to speak with her concerning a position. Unfortunately, the one she'd originally applied for is no longer available, but another has come available that I feel might be a perfect fit."

Kincaid massaged the back of his neck. "I'm sorry. Did you say Sacramento County... *California*?"

"Yes."

The man went on and on, but Kincaid couldn't process anything beyond California. When had Marisol submitted a resume for a job clear across the country?

"Hello? Hello?" Dr. Orenstein said.

"Yes, I'm sorry. I'm here."

"Thought I had lost you there," the man said with a hearty laugh.

He was lost. Lost as hell.

"I'd love to chat with Dr. Chesapeake. I'll give you my direct line for her to contact me, if she is still interested in a position with us."

Dr. Orenstein rattled off a phone number that Kincaid jotted down on a napkin. Once he was off the line, Kincaid stared at the number as if the digits were speaking to him. And they were. They were screaming *Sacramento, California*.

He scrubbed a hand over his head. Would Marisol really consider taking a job in California? Especially when they were building a life together in Indigo Falls? The sound of Marisol's voice pouring through the closed door drew his attention.

How could he give that up? Give her up? He couldn't, which meant he had a decision to make. Give Marisol the message and hope he meant enough to her to stay. Or—

"Kincaid Tinsdale, I love you," she screamed.

A beat later, he balled the napkin in his hand.

Chapter 20

Marisol couldn't put her finger on it, but something about Kincaid had been off for the past few days. The light that normally glowed blindingly bright in his eyes seemed dim. And though she'd asked, exhaustion had been his excuse. Despite not believing that for one second, she took his word for it. Her fear was that she'd done something and, if so, she hadn't the foggiest idea what.

After all of this time, could he have found out about the flowers little Crystal Meyer's father had sent her at the hospital after she'd treated his daughter? In hindsight, she should have told Kincaid about that. It could be interpreted as her trying to hide something. No. If he knew, he would have said something before now. *Right*?

Whatever had him in the dumps, she hoped a good meal would improve his mood.

"Now watch closely, Pixie Pie."

Marisol giggled at the nickname Baxter had given her at age four. At that phase in her life, she was convinced she was a fairy. "I'm watching."

At sixty-something, Baxter hadn't lost his good looks— deep brown skin, towering stature, close-cropped salt and pepper hair. If he looked like this now, she could only imagine how he looked forty years ago. Vaden had to have been the envy of every girl in town.

She mimicked his every move. If she wanted to prepare a feast fit for a king—her king—she needed to learn from the best. And since her aunt had to travel out of town to see a friend, second best would have to do.

For the next hour, Baxter instructed her on how to make mini crab cakes with aioli sauce, arugula and tomato salad with a homemade spicy vinaigrette dressing, beef wellington with a red wine sauce, paired with tagliatelle noodles tossed with veggies, olive oil, and garlic. They finished it up with a chocolate and chestnut torte.

"Good Lord, Baxter. I'll never be able to mimic a meal like this. Maybe I should hire you to come over and prepare the meal. And we can just *say* I did it. I knew you could cook, but I didn't know you could cook...like this."

He beamed with pride. "I taught myself a little something, something over the years. Been trying to convince Vaden to offer a few gourmet options. But you know how stubborn that woman can be." Baxter smiled as if he enjoyed the thought of her stubbornness.

Marisol knew she should stick to minding her own business, but it made no sense for Vaden and Baxter to hide their feelings as if loving each other was a crime. "She'd marry you, you know? All you have to do is ask."

Baxter's expression sobered. "Had a feeling she'd told you about us. Especially by the way you've been ping-ponging looks between us and grinning from ear-to-ear."

"I haven't said anything to anyone. Not even Kincaid."

Baxter chuckled. "We've hidden our love for so long, it almost seems wrong to talk about it out loud."

"There's nothing wrong with something so right. You two clearly care dearly for one another."

"I've loved Vaden Chesapeake since I was a young boy in the fields." He stared off as if reliving a wonderful memory. "That pretty little thing came strolling down that dirt path outside my granddaddy's farm kicking rocks. And when she smiled up at me... *Good Lord*. My heart darn near pitter-patted out my chest. I was a shy boy, but I had to talk to her."

Marisol smiled at Baxter's loving words.

"I fell in love right then and there. Standing behind that rusty mule plow. Yes, I did." The smile slid away. "I'd do anything for that woman. Anything."

"Even marry her?" Marisol beamed at the idea of planning her aunt's wedding. With the help of Rayah and Pinterest—her new addiction, thanks to Kincaid—the event would be gorgeous.

"Marry? Who's getting married," Laz said, entering the kitchen trailed by Jacen. Laz leaned his fit frame against the prep table, his brown eyes narrowing. "It better not be you and Kincaid."

"Better the hell not be," Jacen said. "Especially when he hasn't asked any of us for your hand."

It was crazy, but she loved how protective her brothers were over her. But she still gave them a hard time about it whenever she got the opportunity. "Will you two calm down? There are no wedding bells sounding." A hand came to her hip as she shook a spatula at them. "And if there were, aren't you forgetting I'm a grown woman who doesn't need her overprotective brothers' permission to wed."

"Ha. Keep believing that," Jacen said, swiping a biscuit, then slipping back through the door when a call came over the radio.

Baxter laughed. "Those boys been guarding you like a pit bull from the time you could crawl."

"And speaking of protecting you... What's this I hear about you and Kincaid moving in together?" Laz asked.

Marisol tilted her head and tossed Laz a *get out of my business* look.

Laz waved her expression off. "Do I need to pay Kincaid a visit?"

"You can pay a visit to the freezer and get us some ice cream to go with this torte," Marisol said. "How about that?"

"Ice cream?" Laz asked. "Are you pregnant?"

This sobered her quickly. "Since when does eating ice cream suggest that someone is pregnant?" Now, if she would have said pickles *and* ice cream, then there may have been a cause for alarm.

He eyed her as if trying to decipher whether or not she was trying to hide something. "Don't make me snap Kincaid in half for knocking you up before marriage." He rested his hands on his hips. "Are you on the pill?"

Marisol's mouth gaped open in disbelief. "That's what you should be asking those skanks you bed."

"*Hmph*. She *tooold* you," Baxter said with a snicker.

As hard as she tried to bite back her laughter, she couldn't. Baxter's words made her crack up. Laz wasn't able to smother his laughter either. The kitchen filled with amusement. It was a good thing the diner was closed.

Marisol couldn't help thinking about her belly swollen with Kincaid's child. Every time she saw Nona, her stomach getting larger and larger by the second, made her eager to become a mother. She sighed to herself. It also reminded her that her biological clock was ticking away.

***

Marisol caught Kincaid eyeing her, but it wasn't in the loving way he normally admired her. Enough was enough. If she had to watch him mope around her living room one more minute, she'd go insane. "Okay, Kincaid Tinsdale. It's time to come clean. You've been sulking all week. What's going on with you?" When he clinched his teeth tightly, a wave of concern rippled through her.

With his eyes firmly planted on her, he finally spoke. "I know, Marisol. And I can't believe you weren't the one who told me."

Damn. He did know about the flowers. "I figured as much." She wanted to ask how, but for some reason, the question made her feel guilty of something. Which she wasn't, by the way. "It's really not that big of a deal, Kincaid. It—"

"Really?" He chuckled dryly. "No big deal?" he asked, running an open hand over his stubble.

Okay. Maybe to him it was. "It was completely innocent."

He paced back and forth, his arms crossed over his chest. "Innocent, huh?"

He'd never been the jealous type, so why was he acting so protective? "Yes. This is ridiculous, Kincaid. It was just flowers. It's not like he confessed his undying love to me."

Kincaid stopped abruptly, fine lines etched into his forehead. "What are you talking about?"

"The flowers Roman Meyers sent me." She stood and closed the distance between them. Pushing her finger playfully into his chest, she said, "Are you jealous?"

She flashed a wide grin, but when Kincaid didn't crack a smile, something in her shuddered. With a thousand percent certainty, she knew he would never lay a harmful hand on her, but the hardened look on his face mimicked the one Patrick usually displayed right before grabbing her wrist tight enough to break it and shoving her against the wall. Out of habit, instinct, or fear—maybe all three—she took a step or two back.

"I didn't tell you about the flowers because I didn't feel it was important enough to warrant a conversation."

"What about you applying for a job clear across the country? Does that warrant a conversation? Or did you not feel that was important, either?"

She rested a hand across her forehead. "Kincaid, what are we talking about? I am completely lost. Is this conversation not about flowers?"

"It's about the job you applied for in California."

"The job I applied for in—?" *Wait. He couldn't mean the one in Sacramento, could he?* It'd been so long since she'd sent her resume to the Sacramento County Coroner's Office, she'd forgotten about it. "How do you know about California?"

He started to pace again. "Does it matter?"

She stood in his path. "Yes, it does, Kincaid." Her expression turned sour. "Now how do you know?"

"Clearly, you didn't tell me," he said sarcastically. "The day you were expecting the call from the baby store. Doctor Orenstein called you concerning a position you'd applied for."

Her brow furrowed. "That was like a week ago. You're just telling me now? Did he leave a message or anything?"

Kincaid glanced away.

Toe to toe with him, she said, "Did he, Kincaid? And did you forget to give it to me?" She gave him the benefit of the doubt that he'd forgotten. God, she'd wanted to believe that was the case, but when his eyes settled on her again, she knew better. Her heart sank to her feet. "Why, Kincaid? How could you play with my career like that?"

"How could you play with my heart? Was this your plan all along? Make me believe we were building a life together, then crush me. Again?"

Marisol shook her head. "How can you say that to me with a straight face? You pursued me, remember?"

"Yeah, I remember."

Whether or not intentional, his words came out in a manner that made her believe he regretted the efforts he'd exerted. It was a good thing her heart was already in her feet, because the shards from it breaking would have ripped her chest wide open.

She could have revealed that when she'd submitted the resume, she'd really wanted the job. She could have shared with him the fact that, though she loved and sometimes missed her old career, she cherished her stress-free life in Indigo Falls more. She also could have confessed that it would have taken a pack of wild dingo to pull her away from his side. But instead of saying any of that, she withdrew.

"Was this your way of controlling me?" she asked.

He stopped abruptly and eyed her as if the question offended him. "Controlling you? No, I wasn't trying to control you."

"It certainly feels that way. Your keeping this from me, Kincaid, was selfish."

Kincaid barked a laugh that infuriated her, but she resisted tearing into him.

"Selfish?" He pushed his fingers into his chest. "I'm being selfish?" He laughed and shook his head. "Wow."

He massaged the side of his face like she'd just slugged him. A beat later, he removed his wallet from the back pocket of his jeans, fished something from inside and passed it to her. Dr. Orenstein's contact information was scribbled on the crumpled napkin.

"Good luck," he said, moving toward the front door.

Marisol stomped after him. "Good luck? That's all you have to say to me?"

Kincaid slapped an open hand against the wall. "What do you want me to say, Marisol?"

"You act as if taking this job in California would be the end of us. People make long distance relationships work every day."

Kincaid whipped around to face her. "I don't want a long distance relationship, Marisol. I want to be able to hold you when I want. Kiss you when I want. Make love to you when I want." He paused briefly. "I can't caress you via Skype, can I?"

"Oh. So, it's all about you? All about what *you* want? What about me, Kincaid? What about what *I* want? Which, by the way, you haven't even bothered to ask me what that is."

He brought his hands to his hips, dipped his head forward and sighed. When he eyed her again, defeat was present in his features. "I thought you wanted me."

The raw emotions in his words, the pain in his features, the torture in his eyes, ripped her apart slowly. In a gentle tone, she said, "Kincaid—"

"I should go," he said. Without waiting for her response, he moved to the door, but stopped before making his exit. Over his shoulder, he said, "For the record, it wasn't a selfish act...not giving you the message. It was an act of desperation."

With those words he was gone, taking a piece of her heart with him.

Chapter 21

Kincaid stood in front of the large window inside his office, staring out at nothing in particular. Pressing two fingers into his temple, he massaged the pounding brought on by stress and lack of sleep. All night long he'd drifted in and out of sleep. The second his eyes closed, it wasn't long before his dreams filled with images of Marisol—smiling, laughing, enjoying his headspace far more than he had. His jaw clinched, just as it did every time he thought about how kindly his dreams favored her.

He was not so much pissed as he was hurt. Well, actually, he was pretty damned pissed. And the near week he'd had to process the fact that Marisol was leaving hadn't lessened any of his anguish. Actually, he had no idea what her plans were, and frankly, didn't care.

Bullshit. He ran an open hand over his head. That was the problem. He did care, about her and their relationship. Apparently, far more than she did.

He just couldn't wrap his head around it. How could she just pack up and leave him? Leave like he didn't mean dog shit to her. You didn't do that to the person you claimed to love.

Selfish? She actually had the audacity to call me selfish. She was the one moving clear across the country. California of all places. Who was the selfish one? Not him.

How could he protect her in California? His hands curled into tight balls, and he fought the urge to drive his fist through the plated glass. *Dammit*. Why in the hell had he not considered the fact that the first opportunity Marisol got, she'd bolt.

Three taps sounded at the office door before it crept open. He turned to see Mason shuffling inside. Even though he'd preferred not to be bothered at the moment, he didn't send his brother away.

"Hey, hey," Mason said.

"Hey. What are you doing here? I thought you were taking the day off."

Mason laughed. "Nona *insisted* I come into the office. I think I may have been getting on her nerves." He took a seat in the leather office chair. "Women."

Hell, Mason didn't have to convince him that they were crazy. He'd tried to tell him before that women in Indigo Falls were nuts. "I can't believe she actually talked you into leaving her alone."

"She's not alone," Mason said, then looked as if he'd said too much. "Hey, I'm starving. You free for lunch?"

Kincaid shot a narrow-eyed gaze at his brother. "Who's with Nona?"

"Ah, Marisol stopped by. They were going to select cardstock, ribbon, stuff like that. So, do you want pizza or something else? I'm paying."

His stomach muscles clinched at the mention of Marisol's name. "I'm not hungry."

Mason leaned forward, resting his forearms on his thighs. With a serious expression on his face, he said, "You were wrong, Kincaid. You need to apologize."

Kincaid shoved his hands into his pockets. "I know I was wrong, but so was she. We were building something.

Something real. Something solid. Or so I thought." He tossed his hands up. "I'm done. If she doesn't give a damn about this relationship, why should I?"

"You know you don't believe that. Marisol loves you. Hell, Marisol has always loved you."

"To hell with love. It's a fool's game." When Mason burst into laughter, Kincaid shot him a scowl. "What's so damn funny?"

"You know who you sound like, right?"

"Who?"

"Me. Right after my divorce."

The comparison stilled Kincaid. He was right. Mason had gone through the same motions. Slipping down memory lane, Kincaid recalled Mason's exact words as he watched him stare at his newly acquired divorce decree. "*To hell with love*," he'd said right before swearing to never sacrifice his heart again.

Kincaid moved behind his desk and dropped down into the chair. He reclined, closed his eyes and sighed. "Why in the hell would she take a job all the way in California?"

"Have you asked her?"

Kincaid draped his arm over his forehead. "I haven't talked to her since..." He sighed. "She left me a message saying we needed to talk, but I never called her." Regret gnawed at him, but faded shortly after taking hold. "California. That's two thousand, seven-hundred, thirty-eight point seventy-eight miles from here. Give or take a mile or two."

"Did she accept the job offer?"

"Her and Nona are buddy-buddy. You tell me, because

I have no idea."

Mason flashed a confused expression. "Wait a minute. For all you know, she could have turned the offer down. And for the record, Nona and I don't meddle in lovers' quarrels."

"Why would she have turned the job down?" He slumped in the chair. "It's a great opportunity for her. She'd be crazy not to take the job. There's clearly nothing keeping her here."

"Don't sell yourself short, baby brother."

"I love her, man. And it feels like a piece of me is being ripped away." He pounded his fist against the desk. "*California*. Long distance relationship? Shit, I can barely sleep without her wrapped in my arms. I can't fall asleep with her in my arms if she's in California. *California*. That's bullshit."

"Hmm," Mason said.

When Mason relaxed against his chair and crossed his ankle over his leg, Kincaid saw it coming. That simple wisdom that only Mason could dispense.

"I'm listening," Kincaid said when Mason rested his elbows on the armrests, interlocked his fingers under his chin, and tapped his thumbs together. But before Mason could enlighten him, his cell phone rang.

Kincaid recognized it as Nona's ringtone.

"I told her she would miss me the minute I walked out the door," said Mason.

A beat after his greeting, Mason catapulted from his chair and bolted for the door. Kincaid didn't ask questions, he simply fell in step behind his brother.

Chapter 22

Marisol held a hysterical Nona's hand while assuring her everything would be okay. But no amount of words could calm an expecting mother when she was convinced her unborn child's life was at risk. Every device the nurse had hooked to Nona—an IV, heart monitor, blood pressure machine, pulse meter, and a baby monitor—made Nona a bit more panic-stricken. And when Dr. Holland informed Nona that she'd be hospitalized for at least overnight, it'd triggered a full-on melt down.

Marisol could only imagine the fear gripping her. Heck, she was in the medical field, but she'd probably be hysterical, too. She slid a hand through Nona's sweat dampened hair to help calm her.

"Where...where is Mason?" Nona asked between sniffles.

Good question. Marisol flashed a warm smile. "Don't worry. He'll be here any second. I promise."

Just as the words escaped, the door flung open and Mason raced to Nona's bedside.

"I'm here, baby. I'm here."

Through more tears, Nona said, "They...say...I...have to stay overnight."

"I won't leave your side," Mason said, raining kisses all over her face.

For the first time since they'd arrived, Nona smiled. Mason's touch and words seemed to have a calming effect on her. It was a beautiful sight to witness just how much those two cared for one another. *The power of love*. Marisol wiped at her eyes.

The rustle of the curtain behind her drew her attention. Tossing a glance over her shoulder, she froze. Kincaid stood partially blocked by the fabric. His gaze locked with hers, neither uttering a word.

God, she'd missed him, far more than she would ever admit. She'd fought tooth and nail to not admit it to herself. Mainly because she wanted to be angry with him. At least her thoughts were safe. It wasn't like he could read her mind. Although, the way he stared at her might have suggested he was trying.

"Marisol, what is going on?" Mason asked.

Drawing her attention away from Kincaid, she faced a visibly shaken Mason. Not to downplay the severity of Nona's condition or cause undue alarm, Marisol smiled warmly. "She has a kidney infection, but she's going to be fine. Baby Abigail, too."

Mason blew a long stream of air. "This is my fault. I should have made you come to the hospital last night. But you can be as stubborn as a mule sometimes, woman." He rained more kisses down on her.

Nona rested her hand on the side of his face. "I thought it was nothing. I should have listened. I'm sorry."

Was it wrong to envy what these two had? Wanting something so beautiful couldn't be wrong. "She's getting fluids and antibiotics. They want to monitor both mommy and baby overnight." Marisol flashed another warm smile and rested her hand on Nona's shoulder. "Both of you are going to be just fine," she reassured.

Mason captured Nona's hand. Careful as to not disturb the IV, he kissed it delicately. "Nona Rogers soon-to-be Tinsdale, don't you ever scare me like this again."

"Okay," Nona said in a vulnerable tone.

If there were two things Marisol could say about the Tinsdale men, they weren't afraid to show affection, regardless of who was present, and they loved their women with vigor and passion. Marisol tossed another glance over her shoulder, but Kincaid was no longer there. A sad feeling washed over her.

Facing the doting couple again, she said, "Well, I believe my work here is done. You get some rest," she said to Nona. "And you... I would say not to worry, but somehow I think that would be pointless."

"How about I just not let Nona see me worry?"

"That'll work," Marisol said.

"Thank you for everything," Nona said, the sincerity visible in her eyes.

"Yeah, Marisol. Thank you," Mason said. "I'm forever in your debt."

Seeing them so much in love was payment enough. Marisol nodded and headed out the door, but before she could exit, Mason moved up behind her, calling her name.

"I usually don't meddle in my brother's personal affairs, and I probably shouldn't start now, but he truly misses you. I hope you two can work this out. I don't want to see... Well, I just hope you can work it out."

The part of her that wasn't marred by Kincaid's deceit hoped the same. "Thank you, Mason. Now go..." She shooed him away. "Be with your wife-to-be."

JOY AVERY

Standing in the bright hallway, Marisol closed her eyes and took a moment to gather her thoughts, which were all over the place. How did Nona and Mason make love look so easy? Why couldn't it be that simple for her? What was she doing so wrong?

"You were good in there."

Marisol flinched from the sound of Kincaid's voice. Her eyes flew open to see him standing in front of her. Her mouth fell open, but it took a second or two for anything to escape her parted lips. "Thank you."

He laughed, as if at an untold joke. "I thought Mason would kill us both in his effort to get here. I think we may have mowed down a shrub or two." He laughed again.

Stone-faced, she said, "He was just trying to get to the woman he loves. She needed him, and he was there for her." The jab with her words were intended, and seemed to strike Kincaid right where they were aimed. His heart.

Kincaid slid his hands into his black cargo pants and dropped his head briefly. "I know how that feels. Needing someone more than wanting your next breath and them not being there."

Was that a jab at her? "You're the one who hasn't spoken to me in a week, Kincaid. I called you, remember? You're the one who didn't bother returning the call. I was there. You weren't. You will not put this on me." She brushed past him, taking off down the long corridor.

On her heels, Kincaid said, "Are you the only one who gets to be upset? I don't get to be pissed as hell that you're leaving me?"

Marisol whipped around, her hair slapping her in the

204

mouth. Kincaid collided into her, their bodies pressed against one another's. He rested his hands on her waist in what she assumed was an effort to steady her. His warmth, his closeness, his scent... She'd missed it all, but she didn't allow that to cloud her judgment.

Shoving his hands away, she took a few steps back. "You shut me out of your life. Do you know how much that hurt me? Don't talk to me about being pissed, Kincaid Tinsdale. I'm plenty pissed, but I was still willing to talk to you."

Pounded by a dose of awareness, Marisol remembered where they were. She eyed the two nurses gawking from behind the nurses' station. They appeared to be enjoying the entertainment she and Kincaid were providing. All she needed was for their *lovers' quarrel* to get back to Ms. Ernestine. God only knows what she'd print in that blog of hers.

Massaging the side of her neck, she said in a much calmer tone, "This is probably not the best place to have this conversation."

Kincaid glanced toward the nurses' station, then took her hand. "Come with me."

The sensation of his touch made her obedient. *So much for resisting*. They moved down the hallway, stopping in front of a closed door marked JANITOR'S CLOSET. When Kincaid wrenched the door open, she gasped.

Snatching her hand from his, she said, "What are you doing? We can't go in there."

The idea of being behind a closed door with Kincaid rooted her to the industrial tile beneath her feet. Hell, she hadn't been able to stop herself from following him down the hall. What would she do if he kissed her? Even with her anger, she was fairly certain she couldn't resist his lips against hers.

Kincaid ignored her concern, rested a hand on her lower back and inched her forward. The mild resistance she displayed could have easily been labeled a pitiful display of opposition. Fine, she'd hear what he had to say. But absolutely no way would she kiss him.

Inside, Kincaid flicked a switch and the room illuminated. Boxes containing soap, shampoo, and other hygiene products were stack ceiling high. Metal shelving held towels, blankets, rags, and the such. Mops and brooms were leaned against a corner of the room. A half-empty soda bottle and a crossword puzzle book sat on the small desk against the wall. The idea that the owner of said items could walk in at any time lingered in the back of her mind.

Marisol rotated to face Kincaid, folding her arms across her body. She tried to focus on the vague scent of pine cleaner and not his dangerously close proximity. No such luck when his eyes roamed every inch of her face, then settled on her lips. Each breath she took grew shakier than the last. Her nerves frazzled from not knowing what would happen next.

"I'm sorry," Kincaid said, lifting his gaze to hers. "I'm sorry," he repeated.

The words stunned her. Mainly because they were the last words she'd expected. Especially from the man determined to make her feel like the guilty party.

He took her hand. "I crossed a line that shouldn't have

been crossed."

Why did he insist on touching her? Reclaiming her hand, she said, "Yes, you did. I dealt with that kind of controlling behavior in my last relationship. I won't ever go through that again."

Kincaid massaged the back of his neck. "I wasn't trying to control you, Marisol. You know me better than that."

She shrugged. "Do I? The Kincaid I know would have never hidden something like that from me. The Kincaid I know would have talked to me. The Kincaid I know would have never alienated me."

He sighed and scrubbed his hand over his head. "I'm human. I did the wrong thing for what I thought was the right reason."

"Right would have been you giving me the message and letting me decide my own fate, Kincaid. Right would have been you talking to me about how you felt. Right would have been you saying to me, 'I love you, Marisol Chesapeake, and I don't want to lose you.'"

"I shouldn't have had to say that, Marisol. You should know that I don't want to lose you." He shuffled closer to her. "When you lose someone you love, truly love, it does something to you. Changes you. Hardens you. Makes you fear loss. I'm speaking from experience. If you're asking me to face that fear again... If you're asking me to be okay with losing you again..." He shook his head. "I can't. I can't be okay with that."

Marisol couldn't find the words she needed to respond, because his words sounded so much like goodbye. And how could *she* be okay with that?

Kincaid continued. "I understand your need to leave. It's a great opportunity for you. I know how much you must miss doing what you love, what you trained so long and so hard to do. I know working at the clinic doesn't fulfill you."

She bit at the corner of her lip, fearing if she attempted to speak, sobs instead of words would escape. How'd they come this far just for everything to crumble around them?

"I want to be with you, Marisol. More than anything in this world, I want to be with you. But more than that, I want you to be happy."

The words slowly formed in her head, then made their way passed her lips. "*You* make me happy. And you're right; I miss my job as a pathologist. I miss feeling like I'm making a difference. I miss the joy of knowing a murderer didn't walk free because of testimony I gave." She shrugged. "You're right about all of it. The clinic doesn't fulfill me, Kincaid, but *you* do."

A hint of a smile played at the corners of his mouth.

"Am I upset with you? Yes. Do I think you should've talked to me? Yes. Do I want to lose you?" She rested her hands on his chest. "No. I love you, Kincaid, and that hasn't changed."

Cradling her face between his hands, he said, "Standing here, I've been searching my mind for exactly what to say to you next. I've been searching for the perfect words. You just reminded me that I never had to be perfect for you. I simply had to just be myself. Instead of searching my mind, I'm searching my heart."

"What is your heart telling you?"

"That I was a damn fool to think I could live without. You're my heart, my soul, my peace."

Tears welled in her eyes. "Tell me more," she said with a shaking smile.

"I love you, more than life."

Marisol swiped her hand across her cheek. *This* was the man she knew. *This* was the man she loved with all of her heart. *This* was the man she'd sacrificed for.

"You're embedded in every inch of me. I. Love. You, Marisol Chesapeake, and I don't want to lose you. Whether it's here in Indigo Falls or in Sacramento, my life, my heart is wherever you are."

With furrowed brow, she said, "What are you saying, Kincaid?"

"I'm saying that if you're in California, so am I."

Marisol shifted her weight from one foot to the other. "You would pack up your life and follow me across the country?"

Kincaid smiled. "Woman, I would follow you to hell and back. Barefooted if I had to."

They shared a much needed laugh.

The sacrifice he was willing to make for her was surreal. "What about your company?"

"Mason's a born leader. He can handle things."

It was a few seconds before she could speak again. "You'd give up your dream for me?"

"What aren't you getting," he said in a delicate voice. "I'd give up my last *breath* for you. Plain..." he kissed her gently on the tip of the nose, "...and simple." He followed up with a delicate peck on the lips.

Marisol searched Kincaid's eyes. If there were ever a time she was grateful for the decision she'd made, now was it. "I didn't take the job."

Kincaid's expression sobered. "What?"

"I didn't take the job."

"You didn't— Why?"

When she'd phoned Dr. Orenstein—making up some off-the-wall excuse about why it'd taken her so long to respond—they'd chatted for fifteen minutes before he'd offered her the position, which included a ridiculously enormous salary, a sign-on bonus, and a company car. It'd all blown her away. But what had really knocked her over was the fact that Patrick, of all people, had given her a glowing recommendation.

"As attractive as the offer had been, I chose the most lucrative. I chose love. My life is here in Indigo Falls. My life is with you."

Kincaid took her hand and placed it over his heart, which drummed hard and fast against his chest. Tilting forward, he rested his forehead against hers. "You will never know how much I love you. Even as I tell you every single day of my life and show you in every possible way known to man, you will never know. It's impossible for me to put all of my love for you into words or actions."

Her entire body blossomed when their mouths connected. It felt as if he kissed her with all of his might. Maybe he was right, maybe she'd never truly know how much he loved her... But she had a damn good idea.

The Final Piece of Forever

Months later...

Marisol couldn't believe how time had flown by. She and Kincaid would soon be celebrating one year of dating. Maybe they'd take a cruise or something. Better yet, a trip to Italy. That would be nice.

Diverting her thoughts, she lifted the bouquet she'd caught the evening before at Nona and Mason's wedding and held it to her nose, taking a huge whiff of the white roses and calla lilies. If she hadn't known any better, she'd have believed Nona had targeted her. That woman was such a romantic.

Marisol aimlessly fiddled with the bouquet. She'd half-expected a proposal at Christmas, but it'd not happened. New Year's and Valentine's Day both passed. Nothing.

"What's on your mind, beautiful?" Kincaid asked, dipping to kiss her.

"Just thinking about how breathtaking the wedding was," Marisol said. "Baby Abigail dressed in all white being pulled down the aisle in her custom wagon. The sun dipping below the horizon. Candles everywhere. The river as a backdrop. Just plain gorgeous. And those vows. Those two are so in love. So happy."

When Kincaid eased onto the couch with her, Marisol positioned herself between his legs. He wrapped her in his arms, guided her back against his chest, and kissed her neck.

"Are you so in love? So happy?" he asked.

"Absolutely. On both counts. I'm happier than I've ever been. Probably happier than I deserve to be."

"You deserve it all."

Closing her eyes, she snuggled against his chest, feeling as if she already had it all. "You make me feel secure, Kincaid. My hopes. My dreams. My heart. I know they're all safe with you. I never imagined finding this level of happiness again."

"You sacrificed so much to be with me. Any regrets?" he asked, hugging her a little tighter.

"We're making a beautiful home together. I've gotten my zest for card making back. Sales are starting to really take off, thanks to Ms. Ernestine posting about it. I make my own hours at the clinic. I'm stress-free and head-over-heels in love. Regrets? No way. I've gained far more than I gave up. And I wouldn't change a single thing."

Kincaid kissed the back of her head, then lifted the iPad from the table. "Speaking of cards, I've pinned some you might find inspiring. Rumor has it Janelle will be commissioning you to make the invitations for her grand opening."

Marisol laughed. "You'll take any opportunity you can get to look at Pinterest, won't you?"

"I'll take any opportunity to have you snuggled against me. Pinterest is only a bonus. You're the real reward."

"You really know how to make a woman feel loved. Claiming the iPad, she bent her knees, secured it against her thighs, and scrolled through the pictures. "Wow. This one is gorgeous," she said of the sponge cut and painted to resemble a slice of chocolate cake. "This would be perfect. It's so unique."

"I thought you'd like that one. Your man has good taste."

"Yes, he does. He chose me, after all." She laughed when he jostled her.

"My heart chose you, but I firmly agreed with the decision. Keep scrolling," he whispered in her ear. "There's a ton more."

Marisol oohed and aahed over the unique displays or paper art. Not only did she gather ideas for Janelle's invitations, but also for birthday, anniversary, and graduation cards. She was in card maker heaven. It didn't get much better than this.

"Wow! I *love* the colors on—" She paused and squinted to make sure she was reading the print correctly. Still unconvinced, she brought it inches from her nose. Bolting forward, she slapped her hand over her mouth.

Marisol rotated toward him with tear-filled eyes. "What is this?" Her eyes slid back to the screen displaying a textured black, white, and pink card adorned with silver ribbon and pressed flowers—petunias. In the center of the elegant card scrolled in a fancy script-type font, were the words: MARISOL, WILL YOU MARRY ME?

"What is this?" she repeated.

"They say when a man falls in love with a woman, she becomes his weakness. That may be true, but you're also my strength. You challenge me to be a better man. You've had my back. That means everything to me. You mean everything to me."

Kincaid removed the iPad from her trembling hands and returned it to the table, then snaked off the couch and lowered onto both knees in front of her. Her heart pounded against her ribcage. *"Kincaid…"* The words hung in her throat.

"I fall in love with you over and over every day. I have no idea what the future holds, but I do know that I want us to face it together. I'll never miss an opportunity to show or tell you just how much I love you. Because you've changed my life… Because you've changed my world… I want to change your last name. Marisol Chesapeake… Baby, will you marry me?"

Kincaid's lips stretched into a beautiful smile. If he was nervous, he didn't display any outward signs. *Marry him?* The question stunned her speechless. His every word registered with absolute clarity, but her thoughts were absolutely scrambled. She'd crafted a thousand proposal scenarios in her head, but never had she imagined one so…perfect. The ring—three-stone, princess-cut with pavé-set diamonds in the platinum band—had her captivated.

Say something, Marisol, she told herself. "My brothers are going to kill you for not asking them for my hand." God, had she really just said something so stupid?

Kincaid released a sexy chuckle. "I asked them. *All five.* I'm covered." He winked. "I also asked Va—"

"Yes." Her brain finally caught up. "Yes, I'll marry you. I'll marry you a thousand times."

ABOUT THE AUTHOR

Joy Avery is a contemporary romance author who loves watching her imaginary friends fall in love. When not crafting her next love story, she enjoys reading, spending time with the family, playing with her two dogs, and cake decorating.

Also by Joy Avery

Smoke in the Citi
His Until Sunrise
Cupid's Error-a novella

Dear Reader,

Thank you for your support! I hope you've enjoyed reading HIS ULTIMATE DESIRE. Please help me spread the word about Marisol and Kincaid by recommending their story to friends and family, book clubs, and online forums.

Also, I'd like to ask that you please take a moment to leave a review on the site where you purchased this novel.

I like hearing from readers. Feel free to email me at: authorjoyavery@gmail.com

WHERE YOU CAN FIND ME:

WWW.JOYAVERY.COM
FACEBOOK.COM/AUTHORJOYAVERY
TWITTER.COM/AUTHORJOYAVERY
PINTEREST.COM/AUTHORJOYAVERY
AUTHORJOYAVERY@GMAIL.COM

Please visit my website to sign up for my newsletter and get updates on new releases, special offers, bonus content, giveaways, and contests.

CONTEMPORARY *romance* AUTHOR

Made in the USA
Monee, IL
02 November 2023

45698265R00132